RARE

ANGEL'S DESTINY

DAWN SULLIVAN

Published by Dawn Sullivan

Cover Design: Dana Leah with Designs by Dana

Photographer: Shauna Kruse-Kruse Images & Photography

Models: Brendon Charles and Allison Murphy

Language: English

This one is for all of you who have been waiting for Chase and Angel's story. I hope you love it as much as I do.

RARE: Rescue And Retrieval Extractions

Angel: RARE Alpha, wolf shifter, strong telepathic

Nico: Angel's right hand man, wolf shifter, telepathic, has the ability to see glimpses of the future

Phoenix: Human turned wolf shifter, telepathic, complete badass, loves anything that goes boom

Rikki: Human, kick ass sniper, touches objects that others have touched and gets visions of the past, present, and sometimes the future

Jaxson: Wolf shifter, telepathic, RARE's technology expert

Trace: Black panther shifter, telepathic, badass sniper

Storm: Wolf shifter, strong telepath, has the ability to see into the future

Ryker: Bear shifter, telepathic

Flame: Telepathic

Bane: Wolf shifter, telepathic (other gifts unknown at this time)

Sapphire: Wolf shifter, telepathic, has the ability to see into the future (other gifts unknown at this time)

1

Angel stood outside of Chase Montgomery's house, her hand raised to knock, but she hesitated. She knew he was home. She could feel him near. Her pulse quickened and her body began to heat up at the thought of being close to him. She wanted to talk to him, needed to hear his voice before she left in a couple of hours on her mission with RARE, but hated feeling so damn weak.

Suddenly, the door opened and he stood before her. Chase, alpha to the White River Wolves, father to the two little girls they had basically adopted together the year before, and her mate. A mate she refused to let claim her, even though they had both been in hell for a year now. "Are you going to stand out here all night, or do you want to come in and say goodbye to the girls?"

"Goodbye?" Angel asked in confusion, letting her gaze wander from the bright blue of his eyes, down to the hard angle of his unyielding jaw and firm lips pressed into a thin line. Lips she wanted to trace with her tongue, along with the rest of him.

"I am assuming that's why you're here? It's after their bedtime, and you never come by this late unless you are leaving." There was no give in his voice. No compassion. He stared at her, his face an emotionless mask.

Swallowing hard, she met his gaze. He was right. She'd come to see the girls before she left, but they weren't the only ones. She couldn't tell him that, though. "Yes, we leave soon."

Chase stepped back, holding the door wide open for her. Anyone else would have thought he was being a gentleman, but she knew the truth. He was putting distance between them because he didn't want her to touch him. No contact. It was a rule of his. He had set boundaries because the feel of her skin on his drove him insane. It was something he repeated over and over to himself when she was near, forgetting she could hear his thoughts. "Go on up," he said gruffly. "I will be in the kitchen."

"Thank you." Angel walked by him quickly, then took the stairs two at a time up to the girls' bedroom. Opening the door quietly, she slipped silently inside. The moonlight shone in through their window, landing on Hope's face, where she lay curled into a small ball on the edge of her bed. Crossing the room, a small smile turned up the corners of Angel's mouth as she murmured, "I love you, baby girl." Leaning over, she kissed her gently on the forehead, and then rose to go to Faith.

"Hey there." Faith was awake, and looking at her with wide, questioning eyes. Kneeling down beside her, Angel gently brushed a long, blonde curl away from her little girl's cheek. "I have to go away for a week or two, sweetheart, but I will be back just as soon as I can," she whispered.

"Promise?"

"You better believe it." Kissing her softly on the top of the head, Angel whispered, "Now get some sleep. I will be back before you know it."

The child watched her closely for a few minutes, her eyes slowly drifting closed when she was unable to fight the pull of sleep any longer. Angel waited until she heard soft snores coming from both girls before leaving the room. Heading back down the stairs, she paused at the bottom of them, before turning toward the kitchen. As much as she wanted to sneak out, she couldn't fight it. She needed to see Chase one last time.

He was at the counter washing off a plate, as he stared out of the window above the sink, into the darkness. She knew the moment he detected her presence, because he stiffened, a shudder running through his body. "Are the girls asleep?"

"They are now."

Chase set the plate down carefully in the sink, wiping his hands on a dishtowel next to him before turning to look at her. Angel didn't realize how close she had gotten to him until she saw his eyes darken with desire, his nostrils flaring as he breathed her scent in deeply. "You better go," he muttered, even as he took a step toward her.

"Chase."

"Get the fuck out of here now, Angel," he snarled, "before I forget that you don't want me."

Remorse filled her at his words, and she sucked in a quick breath at the pain they caused. But she wasn't the only one suffering. Taking a step forward so their bodies almost touched, she lifted her hand up, resting her palm on his cheek. "It isn't that I don't want you, Chase," she whispered. "I just..."

Chase didn't give her a chance to finish the sentence. Grasping her hips tightly, he brought her body flush up against his, groaning loudly as he lowered his head and claimed her mouth, tracing her lips with his tongue, and then sliding past them before she knew what was happening. A soft cry left her as she tunneled her fingers into his thick, dark hair, tangling her tongue with his. She knew it was wrong, knew she shouldn't be doing this with Chase right now, but she couldn't stop herself. She needed him, needed to feel his body against hers, in hers. She had wanted him for so long.

Chase growled lowly, releasing her mouth as he slid his hands under her ass and lifted her up, the evidence of his desire pressing into her heat, until she wrapped her legs around his waist and held on. "Give me this, Angel," he demanded. "Just now. I won't ask for anything more."

Her breasts heaved as she tried to regain her breath, and she moaned at the feel of his hard cock against her aching core. She wanted this, and she was beyond thinking of a reason why they couldn't have at least a small part of each other. "No biting."

"No biting," he agreed, even though she could tell that he didn't want to. No, he wanted to sink his teeth into her skin and claim her, but he would accept her stipulations, because he wanted to be buried balls deep inside of her even more. His eyes glowed brightly as he turned and walked out of the kitchen, her body still wrapped around his, making his way down the hallway to the spare bedroom. "Don't want to wake the girls," he explained, kicking the door shut behind them.

Digging her fingers into his hair, Angel pulled him back down to her, moaning when he took over, nipping at her bottom lip before sucking it into his mouth. She felt his hands at her waist, yanking her shirt from her jeans, and she leaned back so that he could slide it up and over her head. She didn't know what happened to it after that, and she didn't care.

Angel let her legs slide down from his waist and stood there as Chase quickly removed her boots, then her jeans. A slow grin appeared when his gaze ran the length of her body, taking in her matching light blue bra and underwear set. "Perfect," he rasped. Angel knew she was far from perfect, but the way he said it made her feel as if she was.

Angel felt her fangs pressing against her gums, her wolf fighting to get free and claim what was rightfully hers. The bitch had done it once before, marking Chase against his will. She wouldn't do that to him again. Angel allowed her claws to extend, swiping at his shirt and tearing it to shreds. Leaning in, she licked at one of his nipples, scraping it with her teeth before moving onto the other. Chase groaned, sinking his hands into her hair, clutching it tightly as he guided her down lower. Angel licked her way down his stomach, and lower still, as she dropped to her knees and quickly got rid of the jogging pants he wore. She licked her lips when his thick, hard cock sprang free, her mouth watering at the sight. "Mine," she growled, reaching out to encircle it with her hand, rubbing her thumb over the tip, and then flicking it with her tongue.

"Fuck, Angel," Chase muttered, tightening his grip in her hair, holding her still. She looked up at him, seeing his wolf in his eyes, knowing he wanted more than she was willing to give him that night. No, she could not allow him to claim her, but she would give him this. Running the tip of her tongue up one side of his straining erection, she rolled her tongue around the top, then closed her mouth and sucked him deep inside, reveling in the barely restrained power running through him. Pulling back, she licked the tip, before sliding her mouth all of the way down again as far as she could go, then back up, moving slowly.

Chase let her have control at first, but then he took over, holding her still as he began to move. She cupped his balls, tugging lightly, moaning as he thrust faster and faster. Suddenly, he stopped, pulling free of her mouth. "I've been waiting a long time for this," he growled. "I'll be damned if I am going to finish in your mouth."

Angel's eyes widened at the fierceness in his voice, and she rose slowly, gasping when he picked her up and stalked to the bed. Tossing her on it, he quickly followed, prowling his way up to her. "Chase!" she gasped, when he used a claw to slice her underwear from her, her bra quickly following.

Covering her mouth with his, he settled between her legs, his straining cock finding her wet heat. She moaned as he slowly began to enter her, need coursing through her. "Damn, you are so fucking tight," he groaned, his arms trembling as he held himself above her.

Angel knew he was trying not to hurt her, but her body was on fire. She needed to feel him deep inside, moving with her. Digging her nails into his ass, she thrust upwards, throwing her head back and gasping as pure pleasure rushed through her. Chase grunted her name as he settled over her and began to move. Angel's fangs punched through her gums, and her eyes locked on his neck where she'd left her mark months before. She wanted to bite him again, even though she knew it wasn't right. She wanted to re-enforce her claim on him.

"Do it," he growled, his own fangs evident. "Bite me, Angel."

"No," she whispered, raking her nails down his back as the pressure began to build inside her, pure pleasure rolling through her as he thrust again and again. "I won't do that to you again."

"Fucking do it," he ground out, grabbing the back of her head and pulling her to him. "I need it," he groaned. "Angel..."

It was a plea, one she could not ignore, even though she knew it was unfair to him. Opening her mouth, she licked her fangs, panting lightly as she hovered over his shoulder. A shudder ran through her as she ran her tongue over his skin. She felt him tense in anticipation, and then she lost the fight, sinking her teeth in deep, unable to hold back any longer. Chase roared as he came hard, thrusting deep, once, twice, and then Angel flew apart underneath him. She felt his mouth on her neck, sucking hard on her skin, before raking his fangs across it, but he never once broke the skin. Even in the aroused state he was in, he still kept his promise.

They lay in silence afterwards, Chase holding her close as he gently ran his hand down her long hair and over her back. Her eyes drifted shut and she snuggled into him, loving how he felt next to her. If only life was different, she could have this every day. But it didn't do any good to think about what could have been. It didn't change the way things were.

Angel waited until Chase's breathing evened out, and his hand on her back stilled, before slowly moving out of his arms. Leaving the bed, she found her clothes and got dressed quickly, all the while wishing she could stay, but knowing it was impossible. When she was ready, she went back to the bed for one last look at the man she loved with all of her heart, but refused to let claim her until she knew her children were safe from the evil that stalked all of them. Leaning over, she brushed one last kiss on his lips before slipping out of the room without a word.

2

The General stood in front of the fireplace in his large, six-bedroom house in Washington. He owned several places throughout the world, but had to be very careful because RARE seemed to be finding them slowly, one-by-one. He moved often, at least once, and sometimes twice, a week. The only place he had really felt safe was in Alaska, but somehow they'd even managed to find him there. He didn't know how for sure, but he did have his suspicions. It did not matter though. Soon he would have their leader right where he wanted her. She would be begging him for mercy, on bended knee. Because very soon, he would have something she treasured more than life itself. Her children. Not just the one that was taking care of some business for him in California right now, but all of them. Jade, the daughter he had managed to kidnap from Angel so long ago, just to have the bitch find and rescue her the year before. The little she-wolf was more like her mom than he'd realized, and he wanted her back. He did not care if she had a mate.

He would give her a new one. The mate bond could be broken. He was sure of it. His scientists had been working on finding a way for the past twelve years, and he knew they were getting close. She would be the perfect subject for them to experiment on.

He was also going to take those little twin brats Angel had found when she raided one of his facilities. He knew she claimed them as her own children, which only made his plans that much sweeter. The bitch had stolen them from him. They were *his*, and he was taking them back.

They would all be punished for leaving him. They needed to learn to obey him. They had no choice. He was their God, and they were his puppets. Just like everyone else under his thumb. Even Angel's son. A shudder ran through the General when he thought of Jinx. The man had power, like nothing he had ever seen before. He needed to keep Jinx on his side, so he'd decided to give him a present soon. One he couldn't refuse. Something to keep him occupied, and happy to do the General's bidding. And if it didn't work out, there were always the iron cells deep in the earth in D.C. where he kept his most prized possessions, including a woman who intrigued him like no other.

The General laughed as he watched the loudly crackling fire in front of him, loving how the flames burned brightly in a beautiful red, yellow, and orange pattern. It reminded him of another Flame, one with fiery red hair, and an attitude to match. He'd lost her to that bitch, Angel, too. Along with many more that he wanted back, like Serenity. He knew she was pregnant with Phoenix's baby. An evil grin stole across his face as he thought about what a prize that child would be. He would have them all back, he vowed. Every last one of them. First, he would start with Angel's children, then Angel herself, and when he had them, the rest of them would come. They would all be his.

His plan had already been set into motion. All he had to do was sit back and wait for it to unfold. "Soon," he vowed softly, his gaze never leaving the brightly lit flames, "soon you will be mine."

3

"Entering the diner now, Alpha." Even though she spoke softly, Sable's voice came over the ear coms loud and clear, full of confidence and purpose.

"Go slow," Chase ordered quietly, taking a sip of coffee before setting the cup back down on the table in front of him. His eyes narrowed as he glanced around the almost empty room. Something was off. He wasn't sure what just yet, but he could feel the tension boiling in the air, almost suffocating him. "She's very skittish."

"Who can blame her?" River grunted. "That bastard of a brother of hers should be subjected to everything that pretty little thing has gone through since her parents died last year."

"I agree," Sable ground out as she opened the door, then walked casually in and sauntered down the aisle in his direction. "Just say the word, Alpha, and I will take care of the piece of shit myself."

Chase shook his head slightly, an uneasy feeling washing over him. "Care Bear is our mission today. We get her out of here, someplace safe, and then figure out our next move."

A short laugh was heard before Aiden snickered. "Care Bear. Who in the hell came up with that code name?"

"I did," River muttered, "because she's as cute as one of those snuggly little things, and...well...she's a bear. So shut the fuck up."

Chuckling could be heard throughout the coms, and then, "What's wrong, grumpy bear? Someone steal your honey?"

"Enough," Chase growled in warning as River snarled obscenities in his ear. "We have a job to do. I suggest you concentrate on that woman's safety instead of her cuteness. I have a feeling this isn't going to go as smoothly as we hoped."

"What's up, Alpha?" Xavier cut in, all business now. "I don't see anything out of place."

"I'm not sure," Chase admitted, hunching his shoulders and bowing his head when a young man walked by, looking at him curiously. "Just be on your guard."

His wolves became quiet, concentrating on the task at hand. He had no doubt they were now surveying the building, and everything surrounding it. The handoff was supposed to be quick and easy, but Chase had learned long ago that nothing in life was ever easy. The past year had been kind enough to shove that fact down his throat over and over again.

Gritting his teeth, Chase looked up and nodded to Sable when she slid into the booth across from him. She returned his nod, and then grinned at a tall, slender waitress with short, spikey black hair tipped with pink who set a glass of water down in front of her. "Thank you."

The woman smiled briefly, a smile that didn't quite reach her dark grey eyes. "What can I get you to eat?"

Chase let his gaze wander slowly around the diner again before replying, "I'll take a piece of apple pie, please. Warmed up, with some vanilla ice-cream on top."

"Make that two," Sable said, winking at the woman. "It has been a long time since I had something sweet."

The waitress laughed, a light, fake laugh, before leaving to fill their order. "That one's nervous too. You could cut the tension in this room with a knife." Sable raised an eyebrow, "Do we abort the mission?"

"Not an option," Chase said shortly, barely suppressing the deep growl in his throat. "Care Bear is covered in bruises under all of that makeup. The scent of her fear is palpable. We aren't leaving here today without her."

Sable's gaze darkened, her jaw tightening in anger. "Why can't we kill him?" she asked softly, hatred gleaming in her eyes. "Anyone who would treat her the way that bastard has, doesn't deserve to live."

Chase gritted his teeth as he replied gruffly, "Because it isn't what we do, Sable. It's not who we are." But sometimes he wished it was. As alpha of the White River Wolves, he had no problem dispensing justice to protect the members of his pack when needed, but the bear they were here to rescue wasn't a part of his pack. Once this mission was over, he may never see her again. It all depended on where she was placed.

"Too bad," Sable responded, fury radiating off of her in waves. Her eyes darkened even more, and he could tell she was having trouble controlling her wolf.

Reaching across the table, Chase covered her hand

with his, squeezing it gently. “I feel the same way you do, Sable, but we are not killers.”

“Then what are we?” she demanded.

A slow smile curved his lips at the fierceness in her voice. “Saviors,” he told her quietly, “and if we have to take a life to protect her, we will. But we do not seek out death, Sable.”

Lowering her head in deference to him, she whispered, “I know, Alpha, but sometimes I wish we could.”

Chase didn’t reply. He honestly did not know how to. He agreed with everything she said, and felt the same way she did, but he was not a murderer. Even though he wanted to hunt down and tear the throat out of every son of a bitch who had hurt all of the victims he and his wolves had saved in the past, he couldn’t.

Shaking his head, he sat back with a small, wry grin. He couldn’t, but his mate on the other hand, she could and would, without thinking twice. He wondered what she would think if she knew where he was and what he was doing right now. As far as he knew, Angel had no idea what kind of business he ran, with the help of a handful of his wolves, and he was going to keep it that way for now. Although, the way she slipped in and out of his mind whenever she damn well felt like it, maybe she did know.

Angel…his mate. The woman who had bitten him months ago, starting the mating process, but still refused to finish it. The woman who rejected his claim on her, even though she had marked him as hers twice now. Granted, he’d practically begged her to do it the last time, but he had to admit, it was worth it.

“Two men just showed up. One is huge. Looks like a mean mother. The other is definitely his lackey.” Trigger’s voice was clipped, short and brisk. "They're coming your way."

Chase raised his head slowly when the door to the diner was shoved open, and a large, dark-haired man entered. He was followed closely by a skinny, very dirty one. He knew who they were, especially the first male. He'd seen his face in the file that appeared on his desk two weeks ago, and then in person days later when he did his recon. That file was the reason he and his wolves were in North Carolina now. It was the reason they were not leaving without the small, female bear on the other side of the diner. "It's the brother and one of his followers." He said follower, because Doug Miller did not have friends. He ran his bears with a tight fist, making sure they all not only swore their allegiance to him, but pledged their lives as well. If they didn't, they died, simple as that. Doug had taken over after his parents died in a car accident fourteen months ago, one that looked suspiciously like more than just an accident. His sister refused to bow down to him at first, fighting him at every turn. She'd even gone so far as to stand between him and a woman he sentenced to death for defying him, which ended badly for both of them. The other woman suffered a long, painful death, and Alanna, code name Care Bear, spent several weeks in bed with numerous broken bones, until she was finally able to shift to help speed up the healing process. After that, the rest of the bears stayed far away from her, afraid of what would happen if they didn't.

"I thought so," Trigger growled, his voice low and deadly.

Chase had gone over the case file several times, and then made a trip to North Carolina to see how things were for himself, before making the decision to step in. At that time, he had filled his most trusted enforcers in on Alanna and his plans. He shared everything he knew with them, along with pictures he'd obtained while assessing the situation. He always gave them the option of sitting a mission out if they wanted to. They may work for him, but he understood that they also had lives of their own. Not one wolf turned him down this time. He'd left his beta and head enforcer home, along with the other enforcers who were not privy to the missions they did on the side, to watch out for the pack. All of the rest were with him.

"If that bastard makes a move, I'm coming in, Chase."

Chase didn't bother to respond to River's declaration. His eyes were on Doug as he waited to see what the bear was going to do. Gripping his coffee cup tightly, he fought the urge to rise and go step between the brother and sister when Doug stopped in front of Care Bear.

"I've got a shot if I need it," Charlotte said quietly.

"Hold off," Chase bit out, his lips barely moving, his gaze never leaving the woman they had come almost two thousand miles to save.

"Get me something good to eat, little sister," Doug sneered at Alanna, his hands clenched into fists at his sides. "And it better be good, or you will get more of what I gave you last night when you get home from work today."

Chase watched as Doug walked past Alanna, slamming his shoulder into hers and almost knocking her off her feet. He took a seat all of the way on the other side of the diner, the other man quickly following. Chase waited for

Doug to scent him and Sable, but he didn't pay attention to them.

"Fucking pig," Sable growled. "I can smell his stench all of the way over here."

Which was probably why the bear didn't seem to notice there were wolves in the diner with him, Chase thought. He had to duck his head to hide a small smile when he saw the undisguised hatred in Alanna's gaze as she walked toward their table. There was still a spark of defiance, not to mention courage, in her deep chocolate brown eyes. Chase's admiration for her grew when he saw the slight trembling of her shoulders, and the thin layer of perspiration on her brow. She was terrified, but also mad as hell. Her long, dark hair swished around her waist when she turned abruptly and stomped up to the front counter.

"Here you go," a voice said softly, placing a plate with a large piece of pie on it down in front of him. Sable reached out and took the other one from their waitress before she accidentally dropped it. The woman was shaking in fear, and Chase knew why. Her name was Fallon, and she was the one who had sent word to his bosses requesting help for her friend. The only friend Alanna had in the world. Chances were high that Doug would go after her first when Alanna went missing. Chase had done his research on the frightened woman as well. She was alone, abandoned on the steps of a church at the age of three. She'd grown up in an orphanage far from North Carolina. She wasn't a shifter, but he suspected there was way more to the woman's story than he had been able to find out. One thing he knew for certain though was that when they left that day, they weren't taking just Alanna with them.

"Oh, crap," the waitress whispered, "I forgot the ice-cream."

"No problem," Chase said gently. "I like it this way, too."

"Are you sure?"

"Definitely." He wasn't there for the apple pie, or the ice-cream.

She smiled gratefully, "I'll be back in a few minutes to refill your coffee."

Chase saw her stiffen and swallow hard when Doug yelled loud enough for everyone in the diner to hear him, "Hey, pretty in pink, why don't you come over here and sit on my lap? We can talk about whatever pops up."

"Well, I would like ice-cream on mine, please," Sable interjected smoothly, handing her plate back to Fallon. "And make sure to warm that pie up so that it melts."

Nodding, the waitress turned quickly and hurried across the room, disappearing into the kitchen. "I want to tear his fucking balls off and stuff them down his throat," Sable murmured, taking a sip of her water.

"What a disgusting, vile creature," Charlotte said softly. "My finger is itching to pull this trigger."

Chase picked up his fork and speared the pie in front of him, taking a bite before letting his gaze wander back to dickhead Doug. He skipped right over him when he realized the bear's eyes were now taking in everyone in the room. There was a darkness in them, one that Chase had seen before several times in other assholes who thought it was okay to mistreat the people who put their trust in you, and depended on you.

Alanna emerged from the kitchen carrying several plates of food on a large tray. Stalking across the floor, she stopped in front of Doug's table and dropped the tray on it, before turning to leave. Doug reached out quickly and snagged her tiny wrist, squeezing it tightly. "We will discuss your disobedience at home tonight, little sister."

Not a word came out of Alanna's mouth, but Chase saw her bite her bottom lip hard to hold back the scream that threatened to break free. He could almost feel her pain himself, and had to force himself to stay in his seat. He had no doubt that if the bastard hadn't broken Alanna's wrist, he'd come damn close.

When one of the customers moved to step in, Alanna shook her head frantically, waving them back. "Thank you, but everything is okay," she told them, with a small smile. "I'll be fine."

Doug glared at the young man, daring him to interfere, but he just backed away and sat back down at his table. Not letting go of her, Doug took a bite of a piece of bacon in front of him, then a long drink of his milk, emptying it and licking his lips. Smirking, he grabbed the side of the tray and upended the entire thing on the floor. The dishes clattered loudly on the tile, and then all that could be heard was the sound of a glass rolling across the floor before it was stopped by a chair. Doug stood, glowering down at his sister. "That tasted like shit, Alanna. You know what to expect later not only for disappointing me, but also pissing me off."

"Fuck this," River growled. "I'm coming in."

"Stop," Chase commanded, even though he wanted nothing more than to rip out Doug's throat himself. "He's leaving. We need to do this cleanly so he doesn't suspect where she's been taken."

"I hate that we can't just walk up to the asshole and tell him she's coming with us and to stay the hell away from her," Sable growled, her eyes snapping with fury.

"You know he won't back down, Sable," Chase said calmly, watching Doug and his sleazy lackey leave the diner. "He will follow her, and he would know exactly where to look once he figured out who we are."

"Remind me again why I can't put a bullet in him," Charlotte whispered. Chase knew her rifle was trained on the two bears as they made their way across the parking lot to their truck. All he would have to do was give the word, and she would take them both out. He was her alpha. He held all of the control. No one disobeyed his orders. Unfortunately, he had his own orders. Even though he ran his portion of the business, he still answered to someone higher up. "I don't see where one little bullet would hurt," she went on. "Maybe just bust a kneecap. Let him see what it feels like."

Chase shook his head, even though Charlotte couldn't see him. "No, let them go." But he could not resist adding, "For now."

"Here you go," Fallon said, hurriedly placing Sable's plate down on the table. Gesturing toward where Alanna was now kneeling on the floor, stacking dishes on a tray while holding her other arm close to her waist, she whispered, "I need to help her."

"Go," Chase ordered quietly, "help her, and then take her out the back door. We will meet you there."

Her brow furrowing in confusion, Fallon questioned, "Why?"

"You asked for help," Sable said softly. "We are that help."

Her eyes widened in shock, then misted over with tears as Fallon whispered, "You came."

"Yes, we did," Chase replied, spearing another piece of the pie that he didn't want to eat. "Make sure and act normal, Fallon. We don't want any attention drawn to us."

"As normal as I can," she promised, leaving to go help her friend pick up the mess Doug had left.

Chase and Sable took their time finishing their dessert. When they were done, they left some money on the table to cover the bill, along with a tip Fallon would never see, and left the diner.

"All clear," Xavier said quietly. "Doug and dumbass are already outside of town on their way back home."

"The two couples and older gentlemen that were inside aren't paying any attention to you," Charlotte murmured. "Neither is the guy at the cash register. I wouldn't be surprised if people dine and dash at this place all the time. I don't think he even bothered to take his head out of the paper when dipshit threw the tray on the floor."

"Nope," Xavier replied, "he didn't even look up."

Chase listened to his team talk as he slipped around the corner of the building and to the back of the diner. Fallon and Alanna were already there, arguing in hushed tones. Alanna turned swiftly when she heard them approach, her eyes narrowing as she placed her hands on her hips. "Look, Fallon just told me that she contacted the Council for help, and they sent you." Chase nodded, knowing instinctively what was coming next. "I can't come with you," she continued. "I'm sorry. I refuse to leave Fallon here alone. If Doug can't find me, he will look for her. You don't know what my brother will do to her, before he kills her."

"Miss Miller," Chase said, mimicking her stance, and cocking his head to the side, "with all due respect, you don't have a choice. The Council sent us to do a job. That job is to get you out of here. I have never not finished a job put forth by the Council, and I don't intend to do so now." When she tried to interrupt, he held up a hand, "Let me finish. You have nothing to worry about where your friend is concerned. There is no way in hell we are leaving Fallon to fend for herself. She loves you enough to send word to the Council, a council she should not even know anything about, and is willing to accept any repercussions she may have to just to make sure you are safe. You don't just leave loyal friends like that behind. You are both coming with us. We will keep you safe."

"Really?" Fallon whispered, taking a step closer to him. "You aren't going to leave me here?"

"Of course not," Sable promised, smiling gently at them both, "but it is best if we get going now before someone sees us."

"My purse is inside," Fallon said hesitantly.

"You won't need it where we are going," Chase told her. "He can track any credit cards you use, or a cell phone. You can't return to your homes, you can't take your cars. Nothing. You won't need anything except the clothes on your back and shoes on your feet. It will be safest that way."

Alanna and Fallon exchanged a long look before Alanna straightened her shoulders and turned back to him. "Let's go then."

4

Tell me one of you has the enemy in sight. Angel held her gun firmly at her side, her finger on the trigger, as she waited for a response. They had been hired three days ago to find the son and daughter of a billionaire out of Los Angeles, California. The teenagers had been kidnapped when their father was out of town on business. When there was no ransom call after forty-eight hours, and no leads, the Federal Bureau of Investigations called in RARE. It took her team two days to locate the missing children, and one to devise a plan of attack. The children were being held in the basement of a large, abandoned school, just two hours from their home. They had never even left the state of California, but she was finding out that was the plan all along.

Negative, Trace replied calmly, but Angel felt the tension through their link. He was just as worried about the teenagers as she was.

Sapphire?

Nothing, came the reply, tinged with frustration. *I can*

sense at least two of them up on the roof, but can't get a bead on them. Same with the one on the main floor.

Shit, they were going to have to infiltrate the building blindly. *Trace and Sapphire, hold your positions. Jaxson, make your way to the roof on the south side of the building. Flame, you take the north. Be very careful once you reach the top. Stop and listen before climbing over the ledge. Let us know as soon as it is clear.* The warning was for Flame. Jackson had scaled many buildings, but Flame was still considered a newbie to the team. As was Sapphire, but when she heard that Angel didn't have a second sniper, she refused to stay home. *Nico and Phoenix, you are with me.*

On your six, boss. Normally Phoenix would be outside rigging the building to blow, but not this time. They wouldn't be igniting any bombs today, not in the middle of a large city. It was hopefully going to be an in and out situation, with no deaths. That hardly ever happened when RARE was involved, but the situation today was different. After she had delved deeper into the Perkins family and realized exactly what was going on, Angel knew they had to be very cautious with how they proceeded.

Actually, I want you with Nico. You two clear the building. I'm slipping into the basement through one of the broken windows on the east side. She didn't need backup, and she did not want to frighten the kids any more than they already were. When she was done here, though, someone was going to answer for what they had been put through. Either from her or the FBI, she didn't care which.

Not sure if that is a good idea, boss.

Angel chuckled softly as she let her gaze slowly

wander around the area. *It's a good thing I'm not asking then, isn't it?*

Dammit, Angel.

There is no one in the basement right now except two scared teenagers, Nico. If they see you and Phoenix with me, they are going to become even more terrified. After everything they have gone through, I refuse to put them through more.

There was silence, and then Nico grunted, *Copy that.*

Angel waited patiently by the back of the building until she heard, *Two idiots up here. We couldn't find them because they are a bit preoccupied...with each other.*

Shaking her head in disgust, Angel ordered, *Tranq them, then move down and help Nico and Phoenix clear the building.*

Done.

That was all Angel needed to hear before slipping around to the side of the building. Fading into the dark of the night, she stayed low to the ground, evaluating each window she came to. Finally, she found one where most of the glass was already broken out of it, knowing if she had to smash it herself it would make noise that could attract attention. Very carefully, she removed the rest of the glass, and after one last look around, she slipped inside.

Found one on the top floor. He's down for the count. I hear another talking to someone at the end of the hall. Moving that way now, Nico told them.

Two on the second smoking a joint. None of these dumbasses are professionals, Phoenix said in disgust.

No, Angel agreed, *they aren't. They are just some wanna-be thugs hired to scare the shit out of some innocent kids. That's why we aren't using live ammo unless we have to.*

What?

It was just one word, but Angel could hear the barely contained fury behind it. Phoenix's mate, Serenity, was pregnant with their first child, and the protectiveness in him for any and all children had risen dangerously high. *Right now, our main objective is getting Nathan and Natalie out of here,* she warned him. *Get control of yourself, or get the hell outside. You aren't going to fuck up this mission, Phoenix.*

She felt his anger, along with the need to find and kill the bastard who had orchestrated all of this, but Phoenix replied, *Understood.*

Second one is taken out, Nico interrupted.

Main floor is clear, Jaxson told them.

I only sense one more in the building, but I can't pinpoint where. Flame's voice whispered through their connection, low and steady. She still had a lot to learn, but was fast becoming a respected member of the team.

That's because he's made his way down here now, Angel responded, as she held herself flush to the wall and closed her eyes. *He's angry because he hasn't seen any of the money that was promised to him yet. He thinks maybe if he hurts one of them, sends a piece of them back to the father, that he will pay up faster. What he doesn't understand, is that there was never going to be any money. There is no ransom. That's not what this is about.*

You know who had these kids kidnapped, don't you, Angel? You know who made them suffer through hell? The barely concealed rage in Jaxson's voice matched Phoenix's now. *Please tell me we are going hunting after this, boss lady.*

Raising her gun, Angel turned quickly, slipping out of the room and down the long hallway toward the voices at the end. *How well do you know me, Jaxson?*

Fuck, yes!

Stopping just outside the room where the teens were being held, Angel cocked her head to the side and listened intently. "Your father didn't pay up," someone sneered. "I guess he doesn't love you brats as much as you thought he did."

"Yes, he does!" Natalie cried. "He's coming for us. I know he is!"

There was a short laugh, and then, "You keep telling yourself that, little girl. That pansy-ass won't be riding to the rescue anytime soon. Don't worry, though. I have something we can do while we are waiting."

"Get the hell away from her," her brother muttered, and Angel could hear the pain in his voice. Someone had hurt him, and they were going to pay.

"What are you doing?"

The terror in the young girl's voice had Angel around the door and descending on the man in seconds. Taking in the situation, her eyes narrowed on the revolver the man held in his right hand as he started to slide Natalie's shirt off with his left. "That wouldn't be your smartest move," she growled, unwilling to let him expose the child anymore. Knowing what was going to happen before it even did, Angel squeezed the trigger on her Glock as she dove to the side, barely dodging the bullet that came her way. She was back on her feet within seconds, blocking out Natalie's screams as she closed the distance between herself and the guy who now lay bleeding out on the floor.

Dismay filled her when she realized he couldn't have been much older than Nathan and Natalie. What the hell was this world coming to when children were kidnapping and threatening other children?

Shaking her head, she turned as her team entered the room. "Jaxson, get a hold of the FBI and let them know we found the children, and make sure they know someone needs to come out here to collect what's left of the bastards who took them. Flame, I want you, Trace, and Sapphire to take the kids to the FBI office and wait there for the rest of us. You do not let them out of your sight, do you understand?"

Flame agreed quickly before rushing past her to get to Natalie. After quickly untying the girl, she pulled her gently into her arms. "It's going to be all right now, sweetheart," she promised. "You will be back home soon, safe and sound."

Angel moved to where Nathan sat stiffly in a chair just a few feet from his sister. He had obviously been worked over, sporting a black eye, bruised cheekbones, and a bloody, split lip. Squatting down in front of him, she brushed a lock of dark hair back from his face, whispering, "You know who did this to you, don't you, Nathan?"

The boy stiffened, his jaw set as he refused to talk. She had wanted to have this conversation in private, but there wasn't enough time. She and her team needed to get on the road if they were going to catch the person who caused all of this pain and heartache in the first place.

Angel waited until Nico moved behind Nathan to undo his bonds before she placed a gentle hand on his arm. "You can't let her get away with this, Nathan. I know you want to, but you can't. She will keep coming back again and again, placing all of you in danger. I know you are just trying to look out for your sister and father, but this isn't going to stop unless you help me stop it. We have to do it together."

"She will kill them."

Her eyes never leaving his, Angel vowed, "I will not let that happen. I promise you, Nathan, I will make sure she rots in prison after everything she has done."

"What's she talking about, Nate?" Natalie broke in. "If you know something, if you know who did this to us, you have to tell them."

Nathan looked over at his sister, then back to Angel. Taking a deep breath, he held his head high and nodded. "Okay."

Standing, Angel held out a hand to him, smiling when he took it. "Let's get you upstairs. Some of my team will get you to the FBI, and you need to tell them your story."

"Where are you going?" he asked nervously.

Squeezing his arm gently, Angel told him, "I made you a promise, Nathan Perkins, and when I make a promise, I keep it."

"I won't tell them everything until I know she's caught," Nathan said stubbornly. "I want proof that you have her first."

Angel glanced at her watch, "You got it, Nathan, but I need to leave now to make that happen."

Nico clapped a hand on Nathan's shoulder from behind, and Angel winced when the boy jumped in fear. "You can trust Angel, son. If she says she will deliver this person to you, she will."

"And we will help," Phoenix growled. "Let's do this."

5

Chase and his team rolled through the gates of the White River Wolves compound just after midnight, utter exhaustion beating at them. The windows on the SUV were darkened, so no one could see inside. His sister, Jenna, met them in front of his office building. When she became the mate of a member of RARE the year before, Chase had tried to remove her from the rescue missions, but she stubbornly refused. She said what they did saved lives, and she would take the secret to her grave if she had to, but she was not stepping back from it all. After hearing her story and knowing what she'd gone through when she became pregnant with his niece Lily, Chase now understood why she refused. He let her continue even though the guilt ate at him that he'd never given her permission to share what they did with Nico. That was going to change. Secrets tore worlds apart, and he wasn't going to let that happen to his sister.

"Jenna, go on home to your family. We have this."

"It's fine, Chase. Lily is spending the night at Serenity's, and Nico isn't here."

That meant RARE was out on a mission of their own. "When will he be back?"

"I'm not sure. I try to never bother him unless I have to when they are out like this."

Wrapping an arm around her shoulder, Chase pulled her close and kissed her gently on the forehead. "When he does come home, you tell him what we do here, sis."

"What?"

"You heard me. Secrets don't make for a healthy relationship. He's your mate. You tell him."

"But the council..."

"Nico is a member of the most elite mercenary team out there, Jenna. He is also a trusted member of this pack, even if Angel is his alpha. I am giving you permission to tell him." When she looked like she might argue again, he went on, "Let me put it to you this way little sis: if you don't, I will."

A slow smile spread across his sister's face, and her bottom lip trembled as her eyes misted over. "Thank you, Chase. Thank you so much. It has been tearing me up inside keeping this from him."

"I know," Chase whispered gruffly, giving her one last hug. It was something he should have done a long time ago, but that damn stubborn gene ran in the family.

"It is all clear, Alpha," Sable said from behind him.

"Get them to the safe place," he ordered, "and then have Bran and Slade take over while the rest of you get some sleep."

Alanna stepped forward, a blanket covering her from head to toe, hiding her identity from anyone who might catch a glimpse of her. Glancing from him to Jenna, she hesitated before asking, "What's going to happen to us now?"

"I meet with the council tomorrow afternoon. They will move you and Fallon somewhere your brother will never find you, Alanna. You will be safe, and able to start a new life."

Alanna was quiet for a moment before she whispered, "What if we don't want to go with them?"

His brow furrowing in confusion, he settled his hands on his hips and questioned, "What do you mean? You aren't having second thoughts, are you?"

Chase felt the tension rolling through her, and when she didn't reply, he pushed some of his power her way, hoping to calm her and make her feel safe. "We can talk about this in the morning when we have all had time to rest," he promised. "For now, why don't you go with my sister and Sable? They will get you settled into a room we like to call the 'safe place' here. No one knows about it except for me, my beta, my head enforcer, and the people you have already met."

Alanna agreed quietly, before turning reluctantly to follow Jenna across the lawn to an entrance on the side of the building. Chase's eyes narrowed when he saw her glance back just once to look at them before going through the door and disappearing. Something was going on with her, but he was too tired to try and figure out what it was at the moment.

"Get some sleep," he told his enforcers, "I will need you all tomorrow. A couple of you will be going with me to meet the council, the others are needed here to guard our new guests." Not waiting for a reply, Chase left and quickly made his way to the shifter hospital in the middle of his compound. He needed to get some rest, but first he would check on Rikki since Angel wasn't in town to do it herself.

Rikki was a much loved team member of RARE. The poor woman had been through her own personal hell for the past few months, and could not seem to break free. After Rikki was shot when they were out on a mission rescuing Trace's family from a known drug lord, Angel had been forced to change her to save her life. They had assumed she would wake up within a few days, however weeks passed and she was still in a coma. After finding out that someone somehow managed to take over her body, not allowing her to wake up and almost killing her, Chase and Steele had managed to hunt them down and kill them. Unfortunately, Rikki still refused to wake up.

A low growl escaped when he thought of Steele Maddox. His mate's ex-lover, father of her children, Jinx and Jade. Shoving it back down, Chase stalked through the front doors of the hospital, grinding his teeth together so that he didn't bare them at the first person he saw. It wasn't anyone else's fault his life was so fucked up. It wasn't their fault that Steele was now mated to Storm, and they had both joined RARE, which put him around Chase's mate every single day. The one place Chase wanted to be, but was never allowed. Or that the young woman he wanted to claim as his own daughter, now had her real father back in her life. Or that his mate refused their mate bond and didn't want him. He could go on and on about his jacked-up life where Angel was concerned.

"Chase."

Clenching his hands tightly into fists, Chase stopped

outside Rikki's door, refusing to turn around to face the doctor. "What?" he ground out, barely holding his anger in.

"She's fine," Doc Josie said softly as she came to stand beside him. "Why don't you go home and come back in the morning?"

"No."

"Chase, you need some rest."

"Don't tell me what I need, Doc," Chase growled in warning. "Trust me, I know damn well what I need, and it isn't rest."

Josie's eyes widened in shock, and he hoped she would just turn around and walk away after his outburst, but the woman had never been good at listening. "Well, then maybe you should stop wallowing in self-pity, be the alpha that you are, and go get it."

Chase froze, a low growl rumbling in his chest as he glared at the woman who dared to stand up to him. "What the hell do you think I have been trying to do for a fucking year now?"

Raising an eyebrow, Doc Josie cocked a hip to the side and rested her hand lightly on it. "Seriously, is that what you have been doing? Because I don't see it, Chase. All I see is you keeping your distance."

The muscle in his jaw ticked as Chase tried to control the fury rising inside of him. "You don't understand anything, Doc."

"I don't? Then why don't you explain it to me?"

Glancing around to make sure no one was near, he lowered his voice, "You don't know how thrilled I was when I found her, Josie. My Angel. My mate. The other half of my soul."

"Actually," Josie interjected, "I do. Remember, I found my own mate."

Raking a hand through his thick, dark hair, Chase said, "Yes, you did. But, he wanted you, Josie. How would you have felt if he refused your claim on him?"

"Chase…"

"She fucking bit me, Josie! She claimed me, but I'm not allowed to do the same. Do have any idea how that makes me feel?"

"No," Josie admitted, "I don't."

Placing his hand on the door in front of him, Chase bowed his head, slowly letting the anger drain out of him as he continued, "It hurts. Every fucking day, it tears me up inside. I tried to understand. I really did. I know she loves her children and would do anything for them." Raising his eyes to meet the doctor's, he whispered roughly, "What she doesn't understand is that I love them, too. They are a part of her, which makes them mine. I want to fight alongside her, Josie. I want to help her protect them, all of them, even Jinx. I would do anything to get him away from that bastard, the General. Anything. I would give my life for him, for Jade, for Hope and Faith. But she doesn't see that. All she sees is how she feels, and what she is going through." Swallowing hard, he rasped, "I want Angel to stand beside me as my alpha mate. I want to protect what is ours together, as one. But I can't make her want those things, too, Josie. I can't make her want me."

Not waiting for a response, Chase pushed the door to Rikki's room open and walked through, letting it swing shut silently behind him. He'd confided in Josie, telling her more than he had told anyone else about his relationship with Angel. As alpha, it was his job to take care of members of his pack. He was there if they needed him, for anything and everything. They came to him with any issues and concerns, and he handled it. Plain and simple. Unfortunately, there was no one there for him. He normally was a private person, keeping his emotions hidden from others. This time he'd needed to talk to someone, and the good doctor was there. Now she was probably wishing she'd just kept walking.

Staring at the beauty resting peacefully in the hospital bed, Chase took a moment to collect himself before he closed the distance between them. Reaching out, he ran a hand lightly down her long, black hair, pushing some of his power out gently, letting her feel his presence in the room. No one knew for sure why Rikki still was not awake, but Doc Josie thought she was in more of a healing sleep now. Her body had been through so much, that it was just taking some much-needed time to strengthen and recover.

Chase stayed with Rikki for just over half an hour, talking softly to her, sharing stories of his precious girls, along with some from when he and Jenna were growing up. The doctor said she would come back to them when she was ready, and he wanted to do his part to make sure that was sooner rather than later. And maybe he was doing it for Angel, too. He knew how much she missed Rikki, and how terrified she was that Rikki might never wake up.

Chase glanced at his watch and bit back a groan. It was late, and he would need to be up in four hours. Leaning over, he nuzzled Rikki's cheek and whispered, "Come home to us soon, little sister. You are greatly missed."

Leaving the hospital, Chase walked toward his house, his mind on the things he needed to do before he left to meet with the council the next day. The first was spend time with his girls, Hope and Faith. They had come to live with him the year before after RARE rescued them from the General. They'd managed to capture his heart from the start, and had quickly become a huge part of his life. The girls were identical twins, but there were small differences, and he could easily tell them apart. Both had long blonde hair, and big blue eyes, with deep dimples in their cheeks. The only physical difference was that Hope had a small scar on her temple that she'd received from one of the scientists when the bastard tried to brand her with something.

Their personalities were the main thing that set them apart. Faith was strong and outgoing, full of giggles and spontaneity. Hope was more cautious and reserved, watching everything and everyone closely. It took longer for Hope to trust, but once she did, she did wholeheartedly.

Chase had missed them terribly while he was gone. He couldn't wait to hear their laughter in the morning and receive some of their famous snuggles. He would start by making them breakfast, like he did every day when he was home. Then maybe they would make a stop at the playground on the way to daycare. The girls loved when they stopped there some mornings and he pushed them on the swings.

Opening his front door, Chase automatically walked over to turn off the alarm before it could blare throughout the house, frowning when he realized it wasn't set. Immediately pulling his revolver from its holster, he crouched low, inhaling deeply. The only people he scented were Jade, Hope, and Faith. Jade was staying with the girls while Chase was gone. Trace was supposed to be there, too, but must have been out on the mission with Angel.

Chase quickly cleared the bottom level of the house, before making his way up the stairs to the second floor. He still did not scent anyone else in the house that shouldn't be there, but uneasiness was creeping up his spine. Making his way slowly down the hall, he opened the door to Hope and Faith's room slowly. Slipping inside, he glanced around, his gaze resting on the girls where they were sleeping peacefully in their beds right beside each other. He'd bought them each their own twin bed, but consistently found them in the same bed every morning. Finally, he had pushed the beds together so that they could be close to one another, but still have their own space if they wanted.

He was getting ready to leave to check on Jade, when he saw something sticking out from behind the bed. What the hell? It looked like a foot. Quickly closing the distance between himself and the girls, he bared his teeth when he saw little darts sticking out of their necks. The sight of Jade on the floor beside Hope's bed, clearly reaching for the girls with another dart sticking out of her neck, filled him with a rage like he had never felt before. Dropping his gun, he shifted quickly into his large, black wolf ready to hunt and kill whoever had hurt his family.

A noise in the closet had him turning his head and baring his teeth, a low growl rumbling deep in his chest. The door to the room opened, and a woman stood there, a humorless smile on her face and a gun in her hand. "So, you made it home before we could leave with Angel's brats."

The door to the closet slid open and a large man stepped out, grinning. "Let me take him, Ebony."

The woman laughed, shaking her head. "We don't have time. Shoot him and let's go."

"Well, shit," the man groused, raising his gun, "I just wanted to have a little fun."

Before he could pull the trigger, Chase was on him, raking his deadly claws across the bastard's soft stomach and then ripping out his throat with his fangs. He had no idea who they were, but they weren't getting his babies. Turning, he snarled, his top lip lifting to show his sharp teeth dripping with blood. He sprang at her, a howl catching in his throat when she pulled the trigger on her gun and a dart slammed into his chest, another one quickly following and embedding itself into his neck. Snarling again, he fought to stay conscious, as he dragged himself over to his girls, forcing himself to rise and stand over Jade as he bared his teeth at the woman again.

"Interesting," she said softly, raising the gun and pointing it at him. "You're a strong one. And they all mean something to you, even Jade. My father is going to want you."

It was the last thing Chase heard before the third dart hit him, and he slumped forward over Jade's legs, losing consciousness.

6

Angel pulled into the underground parking garage at the FBI headquarters in Los Angeles just before dawn, utter exhaustion beating at her. It had taken them close to four hours to track down their prey, and then another hour and a half to slip in undetected past airport security and the three armed men who were supposed to be protecting her, knock her out, and sneak her back out of the highly secured airport.

"You bastards!" the woman screeched from the middle seat of the large SUV. "Who the hell do you think you are? You will pay for this! Mark my words, you will all fucking pay! You have no idea who you are messing with!"

Ignoring her, Angel brought the SUV to a stop close to the elevator that would take them to their final destination, and she could not wait to dump the crazy twit there. Stepping out of the vehicle, she took a moment to stretch her aching muscles in peace, before walking around to the other side and opening the door. Phoenix slid out and stood beside her, his arms folded across his thick chest, a dark scowl on his face. When the woman would have started yelling again, Angel leaned into the SUV eye-level with her and growled, "Shut the fuck up before I shut you up." She was done playing games. This evil bitch was the reason two teenagers, both good, sweet kids, were going to be haunted and scared of their own shadows for years to come. She was lucky she was still alive. When they had caught up with her, and Angel looked into her pale green eyes, eyes identical to Nathan and Natalie's, she had come very close to slitting her throat.

Not waiting to see if she was going to reply, Angel reached in and grabbed the woman by her arm, yanking her roughly from the vehicle. Jaxson climbed out behind her as Nico opened the passenger door and slid out. By the time they made it to the elevator, Trace and Sapphire were already there. Scanning her credentials, Angel waited for the elevator doors to slide open and her team to step inside, before she shoved the pissed-off woman in after them. Turning her back on her, Angel waited silently as the floors went by one-by-one, until it stopped on the number she'd chosen.

She heard the woman's breath hitch, and then a small squeak left her lips when the doors slid open and they were met by two armed men in suits. "We will take her from here, Ms. Johnston."

"No, you won't," Angel replied smoothly, motioning to her team to follow her, keeping the woman in their custody.

"Ma'am, we have orders to bring her directly to our boss."

Angel stopped, turning to look at the young man who had to have just graduated from the academy recently. "I made a promise to a boy and his sister last night, a promise I fully intend to keep." Taking a step closer to him, she placed her hands lightly on her hips which slid her leather coat open just enough to show him that she was packing, too, and arched a delicate eyebrow. "You wouldn't want to get in the way of that, now would you?"

The agent gulped and glanced once at his partner who took a step back from them, before saying, "No, ma'am, I wouldn't."

"I didn't think so."

Not waiting for a response, Angel stalked past the nervous agent, knowing her team was on her heels, and with them was the one person who could possibly tear a small family apart. No matter what happened, Angel knew the truth needed to come out. It may hurt now, but it would destroy lives in the future if the lies continued to grow and fester the way they had over the past couple of years. No, it was better if it was all out in the open now, so that everyone could move on. Everyone except the evil, conniving, manipulating bitch walking behind her who was beginning to stink with the acrid scent of her fear. Good. Served her right. She should be scared. Terrified.

"Where are you taking me?" Angel ignored her, continuing down the hall in silence, turning first left, then right. "Dammit, where are we going?"

Angel stopped in front of a closed door, hesitating briefly when she felt the pain and despair on the other side. Turning, she ground out lowly through gritted teeth, "If you so much as look at these kids wrong, you will be wishing you were dead instead of here at FBI headquarters, Victoria Perkins."

"Kids?" Then the rest of what Angel had said seemed to sink in. "FBI? Why the hell did you bring me here?"

Leaning closer, Angel growled, "Think very carefully about this, Victoria. I know every single thing there is to know about you. Where you come from, where you've been the past fifteen years, who you are screwing, who you have killed." The last was said very softly, barely above a whisper, but Victoria heard.

Her eyes widening, she swallowed hard. "I don't know what you are talking about."

"The girl who stole your man eight years ago? I know where her body lies right now. How she died, and where proof is that you killed her." As Victoria's cheeks became bright red and her eyes darkened with hatred, Angel went on, "That may have been your first kill, but it definitely wasn't your last. I know about the man six months later. The one who ended up with a bullet to the head because you wanted the diamonds he brought you, but took back when he found you in bed with someone else. I also know about the woman from just last year. The one you left for dead on the side of the road, her throat slit, after she threatened to tell your lover that you were sleeping with his brother. Need I go on?"

Victoria's eyes widened in shock, and then she glared at Angel. "How did you find out about all of that?"

"You are going away for life, Victoria. There is no way you are getting around it. But, if you play nice for the next few minutes, maybe, just maybe, I won't tell them about the judge you murdered in Texas just six months ago. You know they love the death penalty there."

Victoria's face lost all color as she stuttered, "There is no way you can prove any of that. You're bluffing!"

When the door opened behind her, Angel whispered, "Try me."

"Angel, what are you doing?" Agent Hanson demanded as he stepped through and quickly shut the door behind him. "You need to get her in interrogation now. We have to figure out who she is and what her role is in all of this."

"I already know," Angel replied evenly.

"You know what?" he asked in confusion.

"Everything." Reaching around him, Angel shoved open the door, her eyes scanning the room. She knew who was inside. She'd captured their scent the moment the elevator doors opened, which is how she had ended up where she was now. She'd almost turned around, thinking maybe it would be better to take Victoria back to the first agents they had encountered, but then she'd tuned into young Nathan's thoughts. *I'm never going to get away from her. No matter what that cop said, she isn't coming back. She can't fix this. I'm going to have to live the rest of my life with Victoria haunting me.* There was no way Angel was turning around after that.

"You're here." The words were low, filled with disbelief.

"What's this all about," Nathan's father demanded, standing and glaring at her. "Don't you think my kids have been through enough? We've been here all night waiting for you. Nathan refused to leave. He seems to think you are going to make everything right in his world again." A muscle ticked in his jaw when he said, "I don't know if anyone can do that, but he says you can. That you promised him you would. So we waited." Without a word, Angel stepped to the side. Michael Perkins swore viciously when his eyes landed on Victoria. "What's she doing here?"

"She's the reason your children were kidnapped, Mr. Perkins," Angel said quietly.

His gaze darkening, Michael sneered, "You did something that put my children in danger?"

"Actually," Angel interrupted before Victoria could respond, "she ordered the kidnapping." Crossing the floor to where Nathan and Natalie sat in shock, she stopped by Nathan's chair. "She had them taken, told the people she hired that you were going to pay a high ransom for them, and then tried to split town, leaving your children to fend for themselves."

Shaking his head, Michael asked in a voice filled with pain, "Why would you do that to your own flesh and blood, Victoria? What if they'd been killed?"

Victoria shrugged, her gaze landing on Angel before looking away. "I was angry," she admitted roughly.

"Angry? What would make you angry enough to do something like that to Nathan and Natalie?"

Her eyes flashed before she spit out, "You stopped paying me."

"Daddy, what's she talking about? I thought our mother was dead?" Natalie was the innocent one in everything. From what Angel found out while digging into the family's history, Natalie had never even met her mother. Victoria left town right after the child was born, never looking back. Not for her children, anyway.

Michael Perkins sighed, rubbing a hand over his tired face. "She may as well be. She left us a long time ago, Natalie. Trust me, baby, she's not a good person. She isn't someone you want in your life." Turning back to Victoria, he said, "I stopped paying you years ago, Victoria. I was tired of it. You had no hold over me or the kids. You were the one that left us. There was no reason to keep lining your pockets with my hard-earned cash."

"But there was," Angel said softly, "wasn't there, Victoria?"

Victoria ground her teeth together, sending Angel a look of contempt before letting her gaze rest on Nathan. "I only took from Nathan what was rightfully mine. I know he got it from his dad, anyway. It wasn't that big of a deal."

"Actually, that's not true," Jaxson stated from where he stood just behind her. When she turned to glare at him, he grunted. "You are nothing to me, lady. I don't care what you think. You sucked your son dry for over two years. That money he gave you? It wasn't from his father. He worked his ass off for it waiting tables every day after class, taking on construction jobs on the weekends and days he didn't have school, and doing other side jobs when he could. Instead of being a kid, he's had to become a man way too early in life."

Once Angel had informed her team about what was going on after they left the abandoned school the night before, Jaxson had immediately pulled out his laptop and got to work, digging up anything and everything he could find on the Perkins family. They never went into a job blind, but this time he dug even deeper than he normally would, determined to do whatever he could to help set things right. Angel knew this story hit close to home for him, and there was no way in hell he was going to let Victoria Perkins walk.

"Is this true, son?"

Nathan sat in silence, his gaze going from Victoria, to his dad, and finally to Angel. Natalie reached over and slipped her hand in his. "It's true," she whispered. "I was always home alone. Daddy was out of town on business trips, and Nathan was never there. So, one day after school, I followed him."

Nathan's eyes snapped around to meet his sister's. "You never said anything."

Natalie shook her head, squeezing his hand tightly, "Of course not. I wasn't sure what was going on. I thought maybe you had done something to get yourself in trouble. I had no idea what, but I didn't want to embarrass you by asking, so I just ignored it."

"Jesus," Michael rasped, shoving his fingers through his hair before turning to face Victoria again. "You blackmailed my son? What the hell is wrong with you?"

Once again Victoria shrugged, and looked away. "I needed money."

"Why did you have them kidnapped? I never received a ransom call. You had to have known I would have paid."

Victoria scowled, looking over at Nathan. "I wanted to scare the little shit. He thought he could stop paying me like you did. I wasn't going to let that happen."

"Victoria," Michael said, shaking with anger, "do you have any idea what could have happened to them? Do you know what one of them came close to doing to our daughter?"

"Guess it would have been Nathan's fault then, huh? He should have paid up."

Natalie gasped, her eyes filling with tears. "How could you say that? You are horrible! Daddy's right, we don't want or need you in our lives."

"Grow up, little girl," her mother snarled. "Life isn't always sunshine and rainbows. You won't last long in this world if you think it is."

Nathan stood, straightening his shoulders, and nodded to Angel. "You kept your promise. Now it is my turn to keep mine." Glancing at the FBI agents who were standing off to the side, obviously trying to decide if they should intervene or not, he said, "This is Victoria Perkins. She's my mother. She's been demanding money from me for the past couple of years. At first, it was a thousand a month. Now it's up to five."

"Five thousand dollars?" his father shouted. "How the hell have you been paying that?"

"It has been really hard, Dad," Nathan admitted. Looking at the agents, he ducked his head and admitted quietly, "I have done some things that I'm not proud of, but I didn't have a choice. She said she would kill you and Natalie if I didn't." Biting his bottom lip hard, he took a deep breath, then went on, "She took me to this old building in a seedy, rundown neighborhood. She shot one of the homeless men there to prove to me that she could do it. He was just lying there, sleeping, and she shot him in the leg, and then the chest."

"Shut up," Victoria yelled. "Shut your damn mouth!"

"I think we have heard enough for now," one of the agents said, making a move toward Victoria. "We will take it from here."

Phoenix stepped up, crossing his arms over his chest and scowling at the agent. Daring the man to try and take Victoria from them. "You will take her when my boss says you can, and not before," he growled.

The agent's eyes narrowed, and he grunted, "Do you have any idea who you are talking to, boy?"

Phoenix raised an eyebrow, "Someone who is about to get a call from the director of the FBI if he doesn't step the fuck back."

"That's enough," a voice said from the open doorway. "Angel, I appreciate what you are trying to do here, but I think it is time we let this family go home."

"No," Nathan cut in, "Victoria needs to go to prison for what she's done. I will stay here all day and tell you everything, but she needs to go."

Assistant Director Washington slipped past Angel's team and walked over to Nathan. Clasping a hand on the boy's shoulder, he promised, "She will, son. She will go away for a long time, but this can wait until you've all had some rest."

"No," Nathan insisted, shaking his head adamantly, "this needs to happen now, and she can't ever get out. Ever. I don't want my family put in danger again."

Angel smiled, "Nathan, there is no way Victoria is ever leaving prison walls after I'm done with her. Trust me." Removing a flash drive from her pocket, she handed it over to the Assistant Director. "Here's everything you need to put her away for good, Sir."

A slow grin spread across his face as he accepted it. "You and your team are just as good as everyone says, Ms. Johnston." Holding up the flash drive, he looked over to where Victoria was cussing up a storm, "Thank you for this."

7

Angel sighed wearily when their plane touched down in Denver later that afternoon. She and her team had stayed in California just long enough to answer the rest of the FBI's questions, and then escort the Perkins family home so that they could double check the house one last time to make sure the family was safe. When they were ready to leave, Angel did something that she had never done after a mission before. She gave Nathan her private cell phone number and told him to contact her if he needed help again; anytime, day or night. The boy was strong, full of courage, and willing to do anything for his sister and father. He reminded her of her own son, Jinx, and for once she was unable to walk away and not look back.

Angel chuckled wryly to herself. Maybe she was getting soft in her old age. Nathan and Natalie were good kids, though. They did not deserve what their mother had put them through. Unfortunately, you could not pick the family you were born into.

Rubbing at the aching muscles in the back of her neck, Angel groaned quietly. The two hours of sleep she had managed to snag when they were in the air just wasn't enough. Not after being up for nearly seventy-two hours straight. Which really sucked, because she knew her head would not be hitting her pillow anytime soon.

First, she needed to check in with the members of her team who had stayed behind, and then she wanted to stop by and see Jade and the twins. A part of her was hoping to catch a glimpse of her mate when she visited the White River Wolves compound. She had been fighting the urge to connect with Chase ever since the night they spent together right before she left. The need to feel that connection was stronger than it had been before they made love. She sighed. Made love, had sex. She wasn't sure exactly what to call it, but she'd had to shove down the memories of that night numerous times, or risk screwing up her mission. She'd almost given in more than once, and slipped into his mind. She was used to connecting with him off and on. Most of the time, he was unaware when she slid inside his head, hovering there for just a few moments, and then leaving again. Angel knew it was wrong. It was a complete violation of his privacy, but she could not help it. It was the only way that she could feel like she was a part of his life, and she craved that closeness.

Everyone thought that she was invincible. That she was able to easily handle anything that was thrown her way. She put up a good front. As alpha of RARE, she had to be strong, capable, and even deadly. She didn't have a choice. Her team needed her, her children needed her, but sometimes, every once in awhile, a part of her wondered when she would get what she needed. She always put everybody else first. Just once, she wanted to know what it felt like to be first, and it shamed her to admit that, even if it was only to herself.

As their plane rolled up in front of the hangar, Angel stood and pulled her bag from the overhead compartment, and then made her way up the aisle to stand in front of the door. The moment they came to a stop, she shoved it open. Instead of waiting for the steps to touch the pavement, she jumped out, landing lightly on her feet. A phone began to ring from the back of the plane, and then Nico's low, "Hey, baby," reached her. She didn't want to hear anymore. It hurt her to see other people with their mates when she was forced to deny her own.

Walking over to the waiting SUV, she raised the lift gate in the back and threw her bag in. Not bothering to close it, she went around and opened the driver's side door. Resting her hand on the top of the door, her gaze slowly swept the area as she waited for her team to exit the plane and make their way to her. They were laughing and joking around, in good spirits because they were finally home. A small smile crossed her lips as she listened to them. She was their leader, their alpha, but it was so much more than that. Over the past few years, they had become a family, one who would do anything for each other.

"I'm looking forward to twenty-four hours of shuteye," Phoenix said, carefully placing a large duffle bag still full of explosives in the back of the SUV and then tossing his other bag in next to it.

"Shuteye, huh?" Sapphire quipped, her bright blue eyes

full of amusement. “Is that what they are calling it nowadays?”

“Well, you have been off the grid for a long time now, sweetheart,” Phoenix drawled. “We do things a bit different now than we used to.”

Sapphire raised one delicate eyebrow, “I highly doubt it is that much different.”

Phoenix laughed, shaking his head. “You just wait until you find your mate one of these days.”

Sapphire held up a hand, taking a step back, “I will leave that mating crap to all of you. Trust me, there isn’t a man out there who would want to have to deal with me on a daily basis.”

Angel glanced at her watch impatiently before looking back at the plane. They needed to leave soon if she was going to get everything done that she needed to before finally getting some sleep that night. Her gaze landed on Nico and she stiffened, alarm spreading through her. He was standing in the open doorway of the plane, staring at them, his jaw tight with anger and a deadly look in his eyes. What the hell was going on?

Nico quickly scaled the steps and stalked toward them, lethal intent surrounding him. Leaving the door of the SUV hanging wide open, Angel quickly closed the distance between them, her team right behind her. “Talk to me,” she ordered. The rest of the team crowded in around them, but his gaze never left hers.

“What the fuck is going on, man?” Trace growled.

“The General has made a move,” Nico told them quietly.

“Go on,” Angel ground out, somehow knowing her entire world was about to be torn apart.

"Some of his men infiltrated the White River Wolves compound," Nico said roughly, a muscle in his jaw ticking, "and he didn't leave empty-handed."

"Who?" Angel demanded, even though she had a sick feeling she already knew the answer.

"Jade," Nico whispered. A loud roar ripped from Trace's throat, his claws emerging from his fingertips and his fangs extending. Angel's heart beat faster as she waited, because she could tell Nico wasn't finished. "She was watching the girls for Chase while he was out of town. The bastards snuck in and got all three of them. When Chase showed up and interrupted their plans, they took him, too."

Angel felt her own fangs drop, and her vision began to blur as her wolf struggled to break free. The General had her babies. He had her mate. He may as well have cut out her heart. Her body shook, and a deep growl rumbled in her chest. A pain like nothing she had ever experienced before coursed through her, and she threw her head back, howling in agony and rage. The fucker was going to die for taking what was hers. She was going to hunt him down and tear him from limb by limb. He had made the biggest mistake of his life, and now there was no place on earth that he could hide. He was a dead man.

8

The drive to the White River Wolves compound normally took forty minutes, but this time RARE made it in just under thirty. It took Angel a good portion of that time to get her wolf under control, and she knew Trace was still walking a fine line of his own. His cat was pissed and wanted out to start the hunt for his mate.

Nico pulled through the front gates, acknowledging the guards with a quick wave, but not bothering to stop. Angel was glad to see the rest of the team waiting for them in front of Chase's office building. Jade's father, Steele, was pacing impatiently up and down the sidewalk, his mate, Storm, nearby. Angel flung open her door when the SUV came to a stop and jumped out. When he saw her, Steele bared his fangs and growled, "I'm going to kill that son of a bitch, Angel."

"Not if I get to the bastard first," she bit out, stalking past him and raising a hand to indicate that all of them should follow. They didn't have time to waste talking. They needed to take action. She had to find her babies before the trail went cold. A shudder went through her at the thought of never seeing them again. Never seeing Chase again. No, she would not let that happen. They were hers, dammit! All of them. And she was getting them back.

Conversation stopped the moment she stepped into the large conference room, her team quickly filing in behind her. She saw a couple of the younger enforcers flinch, and she dug her nails into her palms as she tried to get a hold of the barely controlled rage that engulfed her. The others could sense it, and some were terrified.

A soft cry left Jenna's lips when she saw Nico, and she was across the room and in his arms seconds later. Ignoring the sobs that tore from Jenna's throat as Nico held her close and tried to calm her, Angel demanded, "First of all, I want to know how the General's men got not only onto the compound, but also into Chase's house without anyone knowing. Then, I want to see any security footage you have of the kidnappings," Angel paused as pain swamped her. Taking a deep breath, she continued, "I want to see where the abductions took place, I need all the information you have, and I need it now."

Bran, Chase's beta, glanced over at Jenna, raising his eyebrows as if asking her permission to share what they knew with Angel. A low growl rumbled in Angel's chest, and she stepped forward until she was glaring straight into his eyes. She saw the subtle shift in Flame's footing from behind her and to the left as she moved slightly forward as if to protect Bran, but she did not reprimand her for it. Flame had been in hell for almost as long as she had, refusing to accept the beta as her mate. Defending him now was a step in that direction, and Angel would not call her out on it. "Chase is gone. As his mate, you answer to me, not Jenna. Do you have a problem with that, Bran?"

A gasp escaped Jenna's lips, and she turned large, hopeful blue eyes in Angel's direction as she whispered, "You are claiming my brother, Angel? You are accepting him as your mate?"

"He has always been mine." Angel's eyes sparked and she growled again, her lip curling up to show the tips of her fangs as she looked at the beta, and then each enforcer in the room individually, daring them to say otherwise. "Do we have a problem here?"

Bran took a step back, placing a small distance between them. His eyes still locked on hers, he said, "No, Alpha Mate," as he tilted his neck to the side, lowering his eyes in deference to her.

Something deep inside Angel's soul shifted as the rest of Chase's wolves followed suit. They were all acknowledging her as their alpha's mate, an honor she wasn't sure she deserved, and putting their trust in her. The fact that she and Chase were not fully mated yet, and that there had not been a mating ceremony, did not matter. The White River Wolves were now hers to protect, and she would not fail them.

"Good," she said. Standing tall with her shoulders back, she raised her head high as she looked at all of them. "Now, let's go find my family."

"Yes, Alpha," was the united response.

ANGEL STOOD in front of four computer monitors, anger

flowing through her as she watched a woman with long, dark hair dressed all in black, enter Faith and Hope's room. Jade was standing over Hope's bed, leaning down to place a kiss on her cheek before walking around to the other side of the two beds that were shoved together to do the same to Faith. "Goodnight, sweet girls," she said softly, her voice filling the small room Angel and her team were in. "Your daddy will be home soon. I know he's missed you both very much." Angel caught her breath at the word daddy. Neither of the girls had called Chase that as far as she knew, but it fit him perfectly. He was their father, had been from day one.

Jade did not notice the woman at first, which surprised Angel because not only was her daughter a wolf, but she also had some very powerful gifts like her parents. She should have sensed the woman behind her, scented her, felt her presence. But there was nothing. Faith's eyes opened, and she whispered, "Why does he have to go away sometimes? I like it better when he's here."

Jade smiled, slipping a blonde curl behind Faith's ear. "Me, too," she admitted quietly. "I feel safe when he's here."

"Too bad he's not here right now then, huh?"

Jade's gaze swung to the woman silhouetted in the doorway, a low growl emerging as Faith let out a loud scream. Before Jade could move, the woman raised a gun and fired. Trace let out a hiss of anger as a dart was embedded into Jade's neck. His mate took a tentative step forward before her eyes rolled back in her head, and she fell to the floor with a soft moan.

When Faith screamed again, a man walked into the room, raised a gun, and shot both Faith and her sister with darts, shaking his head in disgust. "I can't stand brats. Why would anyone want them?"

The woman shrugged, lowering her weapon and crossing the room to place her fingers on first Faith's neck, searching for a pulse, then Hope's.

"What the hell are you doing?"

She looked back at him like he was an idiot, "Making sure they are still alive. That was a high dosage you gave them. It wasn't meant for the little girls. It could kill them."

The man shrugged, "Who the fuck cares?"

The woman straightened, her dark brown eyes void of emotion, "The General."

Before the man could respond, she held up a hand and moved swiftly over to the window, sliding the curtain back just enough to see out. "The alpha's home. Hide."

"Why would I hide?" the man sneered, a cocky grin on his face. "I'm not afraid of the big bad wolf."

"Ever hear of the element of surprise, dumbass?" the woman asked as she walked past him and out of the bedroom, pulling the door closed on her way out.

The man's gaze followed her, and then went to the children who appeared as if they were asleep. Cursing quietly, he walked over to the closet door, opened it, and slipped silently inside, sliding it shut behind him.

"I'm going to kill that bitch," Trace muttered from beside Angel. "She is going to die slowly."

Angel agreed, but did not say a word as she continued to watch the video play out in front of her. "Look on this screen," one of the enforcers said, tapping the top left monitor. Angel stiffened when she saw Chase in the foyer downstairs, removing a revolver from behind his back.

Since when had he started carrying? She'd never seen him with a gun before. But she had never really gotten close enough to check either. "We'd just gotten back from a mission an hour or so before that," the enforcer continued.

"Sable," the man next to her said shortly, "she does not have clearance for that knowledge."

"Really, Trigger?" Sable asked haughtily as she reached out to pause the video feed. "She's my alpha's mate. That means she is *my* alpha. I don't keep secrets from my alpha."

"While I appreciate your attempt at maintaining the privacy of whatever mission you were on, Trigger, I have a higher clearance in many different areas of the government than you could ever think of having," Angel broke in. "I work for the FBI, the CIA, even the president himself if he asks, which he has twice in the past. Not only that, but I've worked with the shifter council on several occasions." She saw him stiffen when she mentioned the council, and knew she'd found the division he was talking about. "If you need me to contact the council, I will, but I really don't have time for this crap. Right now, my focus is on my children and my mate."

"Like I was saying," Sable ground out, flipping Trigger off as she turned to look at Angel, "we had just gotten back from a mission late last night. We were out in North Carolina rescuing a bear shifter from her piece of shit brother. We brought her and her friend here, and then Chase went to the hospital to check on Rikki."

"He did?" Angel whispered. He had gone to look in on Rikki? How often did he do that?

As if reading her mind, Sable said, "Yes. He goes to the

hospital daily to see how she's doing. When he came home, he found his alarm system was turned off."

"And no one here noticed anything out of the ordinary?" Nico asked. "They didn't see when the system went offline?"

"These cameras aren't watched all of the time," Trigger explained grudgingly as he reached over to turn the video back on. "Chase installed them when the girls came to live with him as a security measure, but we try to give them all some privacy too."

"I can understand that, but with Chase being out of state, why wouldn't you have someone watching them twenty-four seven until he returned?" Angel demanded. "Wouldn't he have ordered that?"

"He did," Sable agreed, pausing the feed again as she glared at Trigger. "Just like he does every single time we leave for a mission. However, the enforcer on duty didn't think it was as important as our alpha did to keep an eye on them, and he fell asleep last night while everything was going on."

"I want to talk to that enforcer," Angel ordered darkly.

"He's been placed in confinement," Bran said from the open doorway. "He will be dealt with accordingly."

"He will be dealt with by me," Angel stated, not bothering to turn around. Nodding toward the monitor, she said, "I'm ready, Sable." She knew she was going to get along just fine with the other woman. Sable was honest, loyal, and would stand by her alpha to the death. She'd read that much from not only their conversation, but also the brief moment she had connected to the other woman just to verify she was someone she could trust. Trigger was another story. It wasn't that Angel didn't think he was trustworthy and loyal, he definitely was that, but there was a darkness to him that she didn't have time to delve into right now. It would have to wait.

The video began to play again, and Angel watched Chase make his way up the stairs on one screen, down the hall to the children's room on another, and then she was back to the first screen as he opened the door and cautiously made his way inside. It wasn't long before the dark haired woman showed up and then the closet door slid open. One thing was clear right away, they had been sent specifically for Angel's children.

Chase fought like hell, killing the large bastard first and then going after the woman, Ebony. He didn't make it to her before she shot him twice with a tranquilizer gun. Tears filled Angel's eyes as she watched her mate crawl over to the girls. It must have taken everything in him to stand over Jade to try and protect her. The stunning blow came when Ebony whispered, "My father is going to want you." She was the General's daughter. Was she his biological daughter? If so, how many more children did he have out there? The thought scared the hell out of her. They had enough evil in the world already, without adding the General's spawn to the mix.

"He fought for all of them." Steele's voice broke through her emotional misery. "He was ready to give his life for all three girls, including my Jade."

"That's because he considers her his, too."

Angel swung around to see that Doc Josie had arrived while Angel was engrossed in the video, and was now standing next to her mate, Ryker. Her eyes were full of sympathy, as she curled her arm around Ryker's waist and leaned into him for comfort.

"She accepted Chase as her alpha," Angel said, looking back to see that Ebony had left the room, returning moments later with more men. It took two of them to pick up Chase's limp body, and then they were gone, taking the most important people in her life with them.

"It is more than that, Angel," Josie said quietly. "She's your daughter. Because of that, Chase accepts her as his daughter, just as he accepts Jinx as his son."

"He accepts Jinx?" Steele asked in surprise. "Has he ever met Jinx before?"

"No," Angel whispered, the pain and agony of what she had just witnessed almost suffocating her.

"What kind of man accepts a woman's son as his, when he has never even met him before? Jinx is a known assassin who works for the devil himself, even if he doesn't want to. What kind of man could just accept that?" Sapphire asked in wonderment.

Angel swallowed hard, fighting back tears as she raised her head and looked at all of them. "My man."

9

The acrid scent of fear was what hit him first. It was so strong and bitter that it turned his stomach. He tried to move, but his body wasn't cooperating. He was numb all over, and his head felt heavy and groggy. Something was pushing him to get up and fight, but he couldn't seem to move. The feeling of danger was surrounding him, and he wanted to howl in frustration, but all he was able to manage was moving his fingers slightly on both hands.

Suddenly he heard a soft whimper, and then, "Why isn't he waking up, Jade? Are you sure they didn't kill him?"

Faith! Chase struggled to open an eye as he heard Jade murmur, "He's still alive, sweetheart, I promise."

"Then why isn't he moving?" another timid voice whispered. His children were in trouble. They needed him!

"He's just sleeping, like we were," Jade replied softly.

"The bad people gave him more of the drug than they gave us, so it is making him rest longer."

Chase gritted his teeth as he moved first one leg, and then the other. Licking his dry lips, he swallowed again and again to try and get rid of the nasty taste that coated the inside of his mouth. His head pounded, and then his heartbeat accelerated when bits and pieces of how he had ended up this way started to come back to him.

Finally managing to pry first one eye open and then the other, he cautiously took in what he could of his surroundings. He lay on a hard concrete floor, and he could see a row of steel bars several feet away. Shifting carefully, he slowly turned his head in the direction of their voices, fury filling him when he saw his baby girls huddled together in a corner, trembling in fear. Jade held the two little ones close, trying to comfort them, but terror rolled off all three, making him want to kill anyone and everyone who had hurt them.

Closing his eyes, Chase breathed in deeply, trying to calm his emotions. His wolf wanted to make an appearance again, but he needed to think logically right now. He sensed that there was no enemy near to kill, so he needed to concentrate on figuring out a way to get them out of there…wherever they were.

Tentatively, he began to push himself up, his movements very slow and sluggish. He had no idea how he managed it, but moments later he found himself in a sitting position, held up by severely shaking arms. He heard Jade gasp his name, but he didn't stop until he was resting with his back against the cold, hard wall. He tugged the blanket up that covered the lower half of his body, frowning when he realized he was naked. Trying to shake the fogginess from his head, he grunted as pain sliced up the back of his neck and into his skull.

"Stay still for a little while, Chase," Jade told him calmly, although he could still smell her terror. "Let some more of the drugs wear off. You are just going to hurt yourself otherwise."

Letting his eyes drift shut, Chase leaned his head back against the wall, a shiver running up his spine as coldness seeped even deeper into his bones. As he sat there, the night before began to play through his mind. He'd shifted into his wolf to try and protect the girls, which would explain why he had no clothes on now. He must have changed back to human sometime after they filled him with drugs. He was a shifter, so nudeness didn't normally bother him, but he was grateful for the blanket to block out the cold, and so that his daughters didn't get an eyeful of his junk.

Licking his lips to try and help the dryness again, he cleared his throat and asked roughly, "Do you have any idea where we are, Jade?"

At the sound of his voice, Hope let out a soft cry and pushed away from Jade to crawl quickly across the floor to him. Jumping in his lap, she wrapped her arms around his neck and began to cry. "It's okay, honey," he crooned, slowly lifting his hand to run it gently down her long hair. The numbness was beginning to fade, and he was starting to feel his strength return. "I'm right here."

"I want to go home," Hope cried. "Please, Daddy, please take us home."

His heart clenched when the word daddy left Hope's lips. He had taken care of the twins for over a year now, being a father figure and loving them as if they were his own, but not once had either of them called him daddy before. Holding her close, he rubbed his cheek against the top of her head. "I will, baby," he promised, and he was going to do everything in his power to make that happen.

Chase glanced up when he saw Jade move out of the corner of his eye, and then she was beside him, leaning into him and resting her head on his shoulder. Faith snuggled into Jade, but reached out to rest a hand on his arm. "We know you will, Daddy," she said softly.

"I don't know where we are," Jade whispered, "but I do know who has us."

"So do I," he told her, "but I don't plan on sticking around."

"Good."

Chase leaned over and kissed Hope gently on the top of her head, then Faith, and lastly, Jade. They were all counting on him, and he refused to let them down. He would get them out of there, no matter what it took.

THE GENERAL WATCHED as the alpha of the White River Wolves cuddled Angel's children close. There was no sound on the feed, but it was obvious that the man cared for them. Ebony was right, he was very protective of all three of the girls. Even Jade. Interesting. Was it because he was their alpha, or was it something more? He'd been told that Angel was the one who had adopted the girls as her own. That they just stayed at the White River Wolves compound so they would have stability in their lives because Angel was never home. He'd assumed they lived in the alpha's house because it was the biggest one in the compound, and there was no one else to take them in.

It was definitely something more than that, he decided as the male raised his head and the General caught the love and determination shining in his gaze. Could the rumors he had heard from one of his past informants be true? Was this man Angel's mate? He'd shrugged them off when the suspicions were brought to him because, as far as he could tell, the alpha and Angel were never near one another. It would seem that he should have delved deeper. He had almost missed a golden opportunity. Almost. The important thing was that if this man truly was Angel's mate, then he now had everyone that meant anything to the bitch in his grasp.

The General chuckled darkly. He would find out soon enough. The next day they would all be transferred to his facility in D.C., and he had plans for the alpha.

10

Angel walked around Faith and Hope's room, lightly touching their things as she tried to connect with them. There was nothing. Not a damn thing. Just like when she tried to slip into both Jade and Chase's minds. And she had a feeling she knew why. The General had some kind of drug he was perfecting that blocked the line of psychic communication to anyone he held prisoner. He had used it against them in the past, and just like then, he was successful in keeping Angel out of their minds. No matter how hard she tried, there was just nothing.

Leaving the twins' room, Angel walked down the hall to the master bedroom. She paused just outside, a part of her feeling guilty for entering Chase's private space without an invitation. Of course, that was her own fault. He would have had her in there a long time ago if he'd gotten his way. Stiffening her shoulders, she shoved aside her apprehension and stepped inside, shutting the door behind her and effectively blocking out the rest of her team and the pack. This was her mate's home, which meant it would be hers too if…no, not if…*when* she got him back. She had openly claimed him in front of everyone, and she would not back out once he was home. She would share this room with him, so that made it hers, too.

Angel stood just inside the doorway and took in the contents of the room. Three of the walls were painted a light beige color, and the fourth was accented with a dark brown. The drapes that covered the windows were brown and light blue. The large king-sized four-poster bed was made of a dark wood, and covered with a chocolate brown comforter with a beautiful light blue pattern adorning it. There was a tall dresser, and a long one with a mirror. She trailed a hand lightly down the top of the long dresser as she looked at a framed photo of her and the twins. He'd somehow gotten it without her knowing. She was sitting in a chair out back on the patio at Nico's house, with the girls on her lap, and all three of them were laughing. She knew exactly when it was taken, as laughter for her didn't happen often these days. They'd been grilling out, celebrating Jenna's birthday. It was so long ago, but Angel remembered it like it was yesterday.

Biting her lip, she tore her gaze from the photo and continued to look around the room. A large picture on the far wall caught her attention, and she slowly crossed the room to get a better look at it. There was a large black wolf standing at the top of a cliff, with a stunning white wolf at his side. The black wolf held his head high, while the white one gazed down below at two small pups playing in a stream of water, looking as if they were jumping from rock to rock. Sitting off to the side of the stream was another white wolf, smaller than the one on the cliff, a powerful black wolf next to her.

Tears came to Angel's eyes as she reached out to trace the pups, and then the other two wolves nearby. The name Phoenix was scrawled in a beautiful script in the bottom right corner of the picture. Her team always stood by her, no matter what, but it would seem that they chose to stand by her mate as well. Phoenix had painted this breathtaking picture for Chase, and she knew who the wolves in the picture were; Chase and his family, Angel, Jinx, Jade, Faith, and Hope.

One tear fell, and then another, as Angel stumbled over to sit on the edge of the bed. After everything that happened, she was finding it hard to remember why she had thought it was so important to remain apart from her mate in the first place. He had tried many times to tell her that they would only be stronger together, but she'd fought him at every turn, so sure she could protect her children better if she wasn't tied to him, and distracted by the mating pull. What had she been thinking? Why did she refuse him? He was a good, strong, kind man. A powerful alpha who would do everything he could to protect the ones he loved, which he'd proven when he stood over Jade as that last dart hit him. Angel bowed her head, whimpering softly. Chase accepted her as she was; bold and brassy, leader of an elite mercenary team. He accepted her children, all of them, not just the two that lived with him. But she had never allowed herself to accept him.

Sobs she could no longer hold back shook her body, as long, loud howls of misery and despair escaped. The General knew just how to hit her, how to break her. He now held all of the cards. Crawling up the bed, Angel laid her head on one of the pillows and grabbed another one to hold close. Breathing Chase's scent in deeply, she let another howl break free. He was gone, enduring who knew what, and she hadn't even told him what he meant to her. He didn't know that she thought about him day and night. That she touched his mind frequently, but just lightly enough to feel him briefly, and then she was gone again. There was no way he knew how often she dreamt about coming to him, claiming him, and allowing him to claim her. He had no idea how much she cared. How much she loved him. He held her heart, her soul, and he didn't even know it.

Angel had no idea how long she lay there, crying into the pillow that smelled of her mate. Finally, all of her tears spent, she reached up and rubbed her eyes. Slowly sitting up, she swung her legs over the side of the bed and made her way to the master bathroom. After splashing cold water on her face, she grabbed a hand towel and quickly dried off. Hanging it back on the towel rack, she took a deep breath. Gripping both sides of the sink in front of her tightly, she let it out through clenched teeth. Staring into the mirror, she watched her pale blue eyes darken as the anger took over. Fuck the General. He may think he was in charge now that he had her family, but the bastard was wrong. First, she was going to find them and bring them home, and then she was going hunting. When she found the son of a bitch, she was going to take pleasure in killing him...very slowly and painfully. He didn't realize it, but he was marked for death, and his days on this earth were severely numbered.

Her eyes glittering in determination, Angel left the bathroom and made her way to the door. Opening it, she took one last look at the bedroom before walking out and closing the door quietly behind her. She needed to regroup with her team. There had to be a way to locate her family, even if she could not connect with one of them, she just had to find it.

She was surprised to see that the house was quiet and empty. She appreciated the fact that her team and the pack had let her grieve in peace. She'd needed the time to scream out her frustration, and let go of some of the pent up emotion she held in so tightly, but now she was ready. Ready to fight for her girls, for her mate, and for her future.

11

The General's men came for them a few hours later. Chase stood when they opened the door to the cell, a low snarl crawling up the back of his throat. One of the men grinned, tossing some clothes on the floor in front of him, followed by a pair of tennis shoes. "Put those on, mutt," he sneered, "unless you would like to keep walking around with your dick hanging out. Personally, I prefer the pants." He glanced over to where Jade still sat on the floor with the girls, a cocky smile spreading across his face as he leered at her. "You, on the other hand, I would love to see naked. Maybe we can have some fun later."

Chase sprang at him, claws out, and felt a brief moment of satisfaction when he caught flesh and smelled blood. The man cursed loudly, jumping back and slamming the bars shut on them. "You are going to regret that," he grunted, clutching his arm tightly as blood dripped on the floor. Flipping off the others who were laughing at him, the man turned and stalked away shouting back, "The General wants us gone soon. Be ready."

Chase waited until they all left before bending over to pick up a pair of jogging pants, and a long-sleeved shirt. He quickly put the clothes on, followed by the shoes, wrinkling his nose at the foul stench of the male who he had just sliced open. They were the filthy asshole's clothes, which pissed Chase off. The only reason he was wearing them was because he didn't want to freeze his balls off, and he did not plan on hanging out with the General's boys for long. The shoes were half a size too big, and the clothes fit loosely, but they would do.

"I can't read him," Jade whispered.

"What?" Chase asked, looking over to see stark fear in her eyes.

"I can't hear his thoughts," she murmured, her gaze moving past him, and then skittering swiftly around the cell, as if afraid they weren't really alone. "They must have given me a drug to prevent me from using my gifts. I can't reach anyone. Not Trace, Jinx, or Angel. I've tried and tried, but something is blocking me. Has Angel connected with you?"

Chase slowly shook his head as her words sank in. "No, not in days," he admitted.

Her brow wrinkling in confusion, Jade questioned, "Days? You make it sound like she does it often."

Chase sighed, raking a hand through his hair. Facing away from her, he placed his hands on his hips and said, "She does. At least a couple of times a week, if not more. I don't think she knows that I can tell, but I feel it. It's…nice. I like having her there." He didn't like it. He fucking loved it. It was the only time he ever felt close to her. He hated it when she left and he was once again surrounded by loneliness.

"I'm sorry, Alpha."

The shame and guilt in Jade's voice had him turning around and moving quickly across the floor to kneel beside her. "You have nothing to be sorry for, Jade."

Jade hugged Faith close, the child somehow managing to sleep through everything, as was her sister. Her chin quivered, and she gulped before saying, "It's all my fault. Mine and Jinx's. If it wasn't for us, my mom would have let you claim her a long time ago. She thinks she has to take care of us first."

"As she should," Chase interrupted harshly. "Her children should always come first. She wouldn't be the woman that I want to be with, the woman that I am so damn proud to call my own, if she didn't put you first."

"But you have always said you would both be stronger together."

"Yes," he agreed, "and I still feel that way. A united front is always stronger in my opinion. You have to remember, Jade, that your mother and I are both alphas, leaders of our own packs. We are both very powerful alone, just think of what we could do together." Cupping her face gently in his palm, he went on, "I will never fault your mother for putting you children first in her life. She would do anything for you, as would I."

"Because you are my alpha," Jade whispered, biting her lip as she waited for his response.

"No, Jade. Because you are my children, too," Chase corrected. "All of you."

"All of us?"

"All of you," Chase reiterated, and then clarified, just in case she was still unsure. "You, Jinx, Hope, and Faith."

Jade clasped his hand in one of hers, closed her eyes, and nodded. "Good," she whispered softly. "Good."

"They are going to be back soon, sweetheart."

Jade's hand tightened on his. "I know."

"I need you to stay vigilant," Chase told her quietly. Leaning in, he hugged her close and placed his lips close to her ear. "They are moving us somewhere, which gives us a chance to escape. If you get an opening, you take the girls and run. Don't look back. Just get the hell out of here and home to your mother."

"No," Jade argued, "I won't leave you."

"I'm not planning on sticking around," Chase promised, "but if something does happen, you need to put your sisters first, Jade."

"Sisters." She breathed the word in awe.

"Yes." He nuzzled the top of her head lightly before moving back. "They're coming."

Jade's emerald eyes hardened with resolve as they met his. "I will not let them hurt my sisters."

Chase leaned down and gathered Hope in his arms, then offered a hand to Jade. Pulling her up beside him, Faith clutched tightly to her, they turned to face the General's men together.

12

Angel found her team back in the conference room they'd originally started in. Jaxson had his laptop open and his fingers were flying across the keys. Not bothering to look up, he said, "I'm checking all flight plans in and out of Denver for small planes, or anything not chartered by a major airline."

"I'll check all of the small airports within a hundred mile radius."

Angel stepped to the side quickly as a young woman rushed into the room, sliding into the seat next to Jaxson and setting her laptop down in front of her. "Thank you, Becca."

Becca, a scientist RARE had rescued the year before from one of the General's facilities, glanced up at her, her bottom lip trembling. "He needs to be stopped, Angel. He has hurt so many people. I can't stand it. I will put a bullet in his heart myself if I have to."

Angel felt the determination in the other woman and caught a brief glimpse of her thoughts. Walking over, she placed a gentle hand on Becca's shoulder. "Sacrificing yourself is not the way."

"It is a sacrifice I am willing to make," Becca vowed, reaching up to cover Angel's hand with her own. "I refuse to live in fear of that monster. If I can somehow get back into his good graces, I could help you from the inside. We could make it so he never hurts anyone again."

"Bullshit," Jaxson muttered from beside her. "There is no way we are letting you go back to work for that man, Becca. Now stop trying to be a damn martyr, and start typing. We have people to find."

Becca glared at him, but Angel tightened her grip on her shoulder. "He's right, Becca. There is no way you are going back there."

Becca stiffened, but didn't respond. Lowering her gaze, she opened up her laptop and began her search. Angel gently squeezed her shoulder one last time before letting go. There was nothing she wanted more than to get her family back and bring the General down, but she refused to sacrifice an innocent in the process.

"Alpha."

Angel turned to see Sable motioning to her from the doorway. Closing the distance between them, Angel raised an eyebrow. "Yes?"

"We have a problem."

"Talk to me," Angel ordered, shutting the door to the conference room behind her to ensure some privacy.

"A council enforcer is in Chase's office," Sable said, turning to walk down the hall toward the front door of the building. Angel followed quickly as Sable continued, "When he didn't show up to their meeting, they decided to send someone here to see what was going on."

"I don't understand," Angel replied, stopping in the middle of the hall. "Why is this a problem? It is a good thing, right? The women can go with the enforcer, and we can concentrate on finding Chase and the girls."

"I don't think they want to go," Sable whispered.

"What? That doesn't make sense? Aren't they the ones who asked for help?"

Sable glanced back down the hall when the door to Chase's office opened and Bran stepped out looking in their direction. "All I know is that last night Alanna acted like she didn't want to go anywhere else. Chase was supposed to talk to her this morning, but obviously that didn't happen. Come on. We need to hurry."

"Stop!" Angel ordered, gritting her teeth in annoyance. She didn't have time for this. She had to find Chase and the girls.

"Angel," Sable said softly, "Chase takes what we do very seriously. He is the one who talks to the council. He picks out the ops we run, scopes everything out himself first before making the decision on whether or not to accept them. Then he brings us in. If he agrees to take on a mission, it is because he feels very strongly about it. He wanted to save Alanna Miller, which means we have an obligation to that woman and her friend, even if Chase isn't here. As acting alpha, those women are now your responsibility. They need you. We all need you."

Angel looked into her dark eyes, eyes filled with a steady determination, and she knew Sable was right. She did need to finish this mission for Chase. It was what he would want her to do. However, she wasn't one to run from a council enforcer. No, they ran from her. "A person could learn a lot from you, Sable," she said quietly.

Sable's lips turned down into a frown. "Then why the hell are we still standing here?"

"Because," Angel replied, leaning in close, "we aren't the ones that are going to be leaving." Turning on her heel, Angel stalked down the hall to Chase's office. Nodding to Bran as she passed him, she didn't bother to introduce herself to the man standing just inside as she entered the room and walked around the desk to sit in Chase's chair. "Gentlemen," she said, raising an eyebrow as she looked at first Bran, and then the enforcer, "what's the problem?"

"There is no problem, Angel," Bran bit out, scowling at the enforcer. "I was just telling Mr. Reeves that the alpha is unavailable at the moment, and he will get back to him when he can."

Angel crossed her legs and rested her arms on the large desk in front of her, knowing the move made her look deceptively casual, when she was anything but. "Reeves? As in Dominic Reeves?"

His eyes narrowed shrewdly on her. "Angel? As in leader of RARE?" He answered a question with a question. Smart man, but not smart enough.

"Yes," she responded, her eyes never leaving his. "Angel Johnston. Leader of RARE. Alpha mate to Chase Montgomery. And the person in charge when my mate is otherwise indisposed." And the man standing in front of her was *not* a council enforcer. Everyone else in the room was under the impression that he was there because he had orders to take the women back to the council for interrogation before they were placed with another pack, but she knew exactly who Dominic was. Son to Dante Reeves, one of the most respected, and long-standing members, of the shifter council. She knew at well over four hundred years, Dante was one of the oldest wolf shifters around. Dominic himself was pushing three hundred. She also knew that Dominic had become alpha to his wolf pack when his father accepted the council position so long ago. What she didn't understand, was why he was at the White River Wolves compound. However, if he wasn't going to be honest with her, she was not above getting the information her own way.

"I've heard of you," Dominic said, bowing his head slightly to her. "The council is impressed with your abilities, as am I."

"Thank you," Angel replied, as she very lightly touched his mind. What she found just pissed her off, and she quickly slipped back out, not allowing her anger to show on her face in front of the others. "I understand you are here to check on the women who were rescued recently." That was bullshit. He didn't care about the women. All that mattered to him was what one of them could do for him. He'd found out about them through something his father had mentioned in passing, which never should have happened. The woman was important, a gift to be revered, not used and abused. And she was now Angel's to protect.

"Yes," Dominic agreed, and he was good, very good. Even she almost didn't scent the lie when it left his mouth. If she hadn't just taken a quick tour of his very complex and manipulative mind, she may have even believed him. Fortunately for her, she knew what game he was playing.

"Sable, bring the women to me."

"I don't think that is a good idea," Sable said quietly.

"Now," Angel ordered, turning her gaze to the woman.

Sable looked as if she might argue, but instead turned on her heel and left without a word. "Bran, give us some privacy, please."

"I will be right outside." Meeting his gaze, Angel nodded in understanding. He might be willing to leave the room, but he wasn't going far. He would be there if she needed him. With one last look at Dominic, Bran left the room, slamming the door shut behind him. She could feel his anger, but knew he would never disobey a direct order from his alpha. And right now, that was her.

Angel stood, placing her hands lightly on her hips, her legs spread slightly apart. Fury rolled off her in waves as she ground out, "Just what the hell do you think you are doing?"

Dominic walked over to the window, his back to her, gazing out into the darkness. "I'm not sure I know what you mean?"

"You know damn well what I am talking about, Dominic Reeves," she replied in a low voice. "You come here portraying yourself as an enforcer, which we both know you are not." When he shifted to look at her in surprise, she snapped, "Yes, I know who you are, and I know exactly why you are here."

Dominic sighed, turning to face her, "Look Angel…"

Suddenly, the door opened and Nico and Phoenix walked in, not bothering to close it behind them. Each took a position near Angel, their eyes cold and unyielding as they stared at Dominic. Bran stood right outside, watching, his arms folded over his thick chest.

"No, you look," Angel growled, walking over to stand directly in front of Dominic, uncaring who was witnessing their discussion now. Before, she had thought to settle this quietly and send him on his way, but now she was just pissed. She had given him a chance to come clean, and she wasn't giving him a second one. "These people, this pack, they are my family now. You will not use them, or the women you supposedly just want to protect, for your own personal agenda. I won't allow it."

"The council..."

"Don't you dare try and throw the council in my face," Angel snarled. "I know this is you, not them." Taking a step closer, she went on, "Trust me, I don't give a shit who you are, or who you are related to, you do not want to go against me." Letting her fangs drop and her eyes go wolf as the full extent of her power radiated around her, she ground out, "Stay away from my pack, Dominic Reeves. Or you will answer to me, and not even the council will be able to save you. Do you understand?"

For the first time since she had walked into the room, Dominic let his anger show. "Dammit, Angel, I need that bear!"

Angel heard a soft gasp from the open doorway, but her eyes never left the man in front of her. "Both of these women are under my protection now. They are a part of the White River Wolves pack, and no one, and I mean *no one* will touch them." When Dominic glanced over to the women, his feet shifting slightly, she grinned, "Do it. I dare you. See what happens when you fuck with what's mine."

Glaring at her, Dominic snarled, "This isn't over, Angel."

Angel didn't bother responding. She knew it wasn't, and she didn't blame him. Dominic was a good man, and an even better alpha. He was just trying to protect someone he loved, and he thought one of the women Chase had rescued could help. Unfortunately, it would put the woman in danger, and Angel could not allow that. She let him get to the door before she said softly, "Dominic." He stopped, keeping his back to her, stiff and unyielding. "If you need help, all you have to do is ask."

He stood proudly, shoulders back, head held high, as he replied, "There's nothing you can do to help if you won't let me have the bear."

"Not going to happen."

She watched as he looked down at the young woman standing just a few feet from him, before turning and leaving without another word.

"He's in so much pain," the woman whispered, reaching out as if to tell him to stop.

"There is nothing you can do for him. His pain runs far deeper than anything you can fix, sweet bear."

She turned to look at Angel, her eyes wide, "You know?"

Angel smiled gently, motioning toward the two chairs in front of the desk. "Your secret is safe here. Please, have a seat."

"Where is Chase?"

Angel felt a small, painful twinge in the vicinity of her heart as she rested a hip against the desk. "He isn't here right now. I'm Angel, his mate, and I'm going to make sure you are taken care of until he returns."

"We heard," the bear said softly. "Thank you."

"What are your names?"

They looked at each other in confusion before the one with the pink hair asked, "If you are Chase's mate, shouldn't you know that already?"

That small twinge became a sharp pang as she replied, "Even mates have secrets sometimes."

"You're in a lot of pain, too," the bear whispered. "So much, that it's almost crushing you. Please, let me help."

"No," Angel refused. "I need to feel the pain. It will make me fight harder."

"She's like Serenity," Phoenix said in awe.

When the bear's eyes turned to him in surprise, Angel murmured, "Similar, yes. Now, your names?"

"I'm Alanna Miller," the bear said quietly, "and this is my friend, Fallon."

"I asked the council for help," Fallon spoke for the first time. "I needed to get Alanna away from her brother. He was hurting her. Abusing her both physically and emotionally. It had to be stopped."

"Does he know about your gifts, Alanna?" Angel asked quietly.

Alanna glanced around the room, then ducked her head, seeming to close in on herself before replying, "Not all of them, but some, yes."

"He isn't just going to let you go, is he?"

"No," Alanna whispered, so low Angel almost didn't hear it.

Angel moved to stand beside her, placing a gentle hand on her shoulder, "You are safe now, Alanna. You are under not only my protection but the protection of the entire pack. You do not have to be afraid."

"A part of me is terrified," Alanna admitted.

"And the other part?" Angel asked, knowing what the answer would be.

Alanna lifted her head, her dark brown eyes sparking as she snapped, "The other part of me wants to go back and kick that brother of mine in the balls. Unfortunately, he's bigger and meaner than I am, so it always ends badly when I try."

The room filled with laughter, and a small smile lifted the corners of Angel's mouth. "Tell me, do you wish to stay here?"

"Is that an option?"

"I am making it one."

Alanna glanced at her friend, then back at Angel, "Yes, please. We want to stay."

"Good." Taking out her cell phone, Angel quickly found the number she wanted. Pressing send, she waited for someone to answer. When they did, she said, "Angel Johnston for the council, please."

Alanna's eyes widened in shock and she sat forward on the edge of her chair. "The council?" she mouthed in alarm.

Angel nodded, leaning a hip against the desk again, as she waited for the council's secretary to pick up. "Hello, Charlene. It is good to speak to you again."

"Likewise," came the elegant response. "To what do we owe the pleasure, Ms. Johnston?"

"I am calling regarding Chase Montgomery."

"Yes?" Charlene's reply was short and guarded.

"My mate is unable to meet with you at this time," Angel said, "so I am calling on his behalf."

"Your mate?" The shock in Charlene's voice was obvious, as was the tinge of jealousy.

"Yes, my mate." The need to get back to looking for Chase and her children was pushing at her, and it was a struggle to stay civil toward the other woman. "He acquired the two lovely ladies you sent him to get yesterday. They are with me now, and both have chosen to become a part of our pack, so they will stay here."

"Oh! We normally don't do things like that Ms. Johnston," Charlene stated. "I'm sorry. You will need to bring them here so that we can find a suitable place for them."

"Are you insinuating that my pack is not suitable?" Angel asked, her tone low and deadly.

"Well, no," the woman hedged.

"I think I need to speak with an actual member of the council, please."

"That's not necessary," Charlene protested.

"It is very necessary," Angel growled. "Put one of them on. Now." She was done. She did not have time for this crap. She was out of patience, and Charlene was about to understand why it was a bad idea to piss her off.

Luckily for Charlene, she was smart enough to know when it was time to give in on her end. "One moment, please."

Bran and the two women were staring at her in shock, but Nico and Phoenix were unfazed. They were used to dealing with her, and knew she did not bow down to anyone, not even the council.

"What can we do for you, Angel?"

Angel smiled when she heard none other than Dante Reeves answer the phone this time. "Dante, so nice to speak with you again." And it was. Dante was always kind and courteous, unless forced to be otherwise. She respected him, and knew the feeling was mutual.

"You as well, my dear. I hear you and the White River Wolves alpha have mated?"

"Chase is my mate," she said evasively, because technically they were not fully mated yet, and while she may not bow down to the council, she refused to flat out lie to them.

"Very good," Dante replied, and she could hear the approval in his voice. "And Chase and his team acquired the young bear we sent them after?"

"Yes, she and her friend are right here, Councilman." She looked over to see Alanna biting her bottom lip in agitation and worry, and she smiled at her hoping to put her at ease. "They have requested a place in our pack," she continued, "and I have granted that request."

There was complete silence on the other line, and then, "Angel, she needs special care and protection."

"Which my mate and I are fully prepared to give her," Angel countered smoothly. "I have claimed her as one of my own."

There was a moment before there was a response, and Angel could hear the members of the council talking rapidly in the background. She could not make out the words, but she did not have long to wait. "The request has been approved," Dante finally said. "We had been trying to decide where to send her, to be honest, but it has been difficult finding a place that we thought would accept her and her unique abilities."

"Thank you, Dante. We will take good care of her here."

"I know you will, Angel." He hesitated briefly before asking in concern, "Is Chase okay? He never misses a check-in time."

"He will be," Angel promised, before ending the call.

"We are putting you in danger," Alanna whispered. "My brother will never stop looking for me. There are things you don't know. Things I need to tell you."

"Alanna," Fallon interrupted. "We agreed."

"Everything is different now, Fallon. When you become a part of a pack like we are, there can be no secrets from your alpha."

"You kept them from Doug," Fallon reminded her, with a sideways glance at Angel.

"That was different. Doug would have used them against me."

"And how do you know they won't?" Fallon hissed.

"Because I do," Alanna said simply.

"She's right, Fallon," Angel interjected. "I know you have been through a lot, and I don't expect you to trust any of us right away, but you will learn to. And we will talk, Alanna, but it is going to have to wait. Just know, you are safe here. The pack will protect you while I'm gone."

"You're leaving?"

"I don't have a choice." Turning to Bran, she said, "Take care of them, Bran. I want two enforcers that you trust with your life with them at all times. It is best to keep them hidden away for now, just until I'm back." Walking to the door, she paused and looked back at the women, "I don't know how long I will be. Bran will be in charge while I am gone. You let him know if you need anything."

"Where are you going?" Alanna asked softly.

"To find my mate."

13

They had been traveling in the back of a cargo van for at least a couple of hours when it suddenly came to a stop. Chase stiffened when he heard what sounded like a helicopter outside. He had no idea where they were, but somehow he knew deep down, if they got on that chopper, it would be the end for them. There was no way in hell he was going to allow that to happen.

"Don't go far," one of the men teased, before opening the back door and hopping out, quickly followed by the other two. He slammed the door shut, leaving Chase and the girls alone in the dark.

The driver glanced back at them as he opened his door, the overhead light flashing for a brief moment. Chase watched an evil grin spread across his face as he said, "Say your goodbyes now while you can. Soon you will be in the air, and once you reach your destination, one will go one way, while the others go somewhere else." With a harsh laugh, he stepped out of the van, slamming the door shut behind him.

"No," Jade gasped. "They can't split us up, Chase."

"They won't have to," Chase told her, leaning down to place a kiss on the top of Hope's head as he hugged her close. "We aren't going to give them the chance."

"What's your plan?" Jade asked, her voice filled with worry and resolve.

"Easy," he said with a grin, leaning over to place a kiss on Faith's cheek, and then Jade's. "When I tell you to, you run. Take the girls as far away as you can. Get the hell out of here. I will do the rest."

"No, Chase. I won't leave you."

"You can, and you will. That's a direct order from your alpha." He knew she was going to argue, but he stopped her before she could. "Jade, you girls are my first priority. I will fight like hell to get free and follow you, but if I know you have your sisters, if I know you are all safe, I can withstand anything. You get to your mother, and then she will find me."

"But I have no idea where they are taking you!" she protested. "I can't use my gifts. They've blocked them with their drugs."

"Angel will find me," Chase promised. "I have no doubt."

"Daddy, no," Hope whimpered, pressing closer to him. "Don't leave us."

"Jade will take care of you, honey. You have to listen to her. Do everything she says, okay?"

Faith looked up at him, her big blue eyes full of fear, "No, please."

"It's going to be okay," he told her, running a hand gently down her cheek. "Now, I want you all to shift quickly. And when they open the back doors, run. I will take care of the rest."

"How?" Jade asked incredulously as she looked at the chains wrapped tightly around his wrists. They hadn't bothered to chain up Jade or the twins, thinking they were no threat, but there was no way to break the bindings on Chase.

"Just do it," he ordered. "Trust me." The bastards had wound the chains around his wrists tightly, but left his legs free so that he could walk to the van. There was no way he could shift, but that didn't mean he was unable to fight. Hearing a noise just outside the back door, he urged, "Hurry!"

Hope and Faith shifted first, leaving their nightgowns on the floor of the van. Jade reluctantly was next. He knew there would be guns trained on the van. There was no way they had left it unattended. But this was their one and only chance, and he refused to give up until his daughters were free. "Get ready," he said softly, "and run fast. Really fast. Follow Jade."

Jade whined plaintively, and he smiled at her. "Take care of your sisters, sweetheart. I love all of you, so much."

The door swung open, and Chase sprang from the floor. He was out of the van and half-way shifted, swiping his claws across the man's throat. He cursed, wishing he could fully change, but the chains prevented it. He was aware of Jade and the girls slipping out of the van and underneath it while he distracted the men that came at him. He needed to keep the soldiers distracted. He knew Jade was looking for the best way out without drawing attention their way.

Men came at him from all directions, but Chase didn't

back down. Fighting with his hands bound was difficult, but not impossible, and he would do whatever it took to get his children free. He refused to let the General have them.

Chase felt the first bullet enter his leg, and he dropped to one knee, but blocked out the pain, getting right back up and taking out two more men. The second bullet went through his shoulder, and the third in his upper arm. They weren't messing around. No tranquilizers this time. These bullets tore through his flesh, causing excruciating pain, but he fought on. A loud roar left him as he sprang on his next victim, pulling him to the ground and snapping his neck, before rising again to go after the next one. It wasn't until the fourth bullet hit him that he fell to his knees, struggling to get back up. Blood flowed from his wounds, and he roared again in pain and anger. He'd managed to take out six of his enemies, but he wanted more. He wanted them all dead.

Someone slammed something into the back of his head, and he grunted as he slumped over into the dirt. Pushing back up, he swiped at the bastard behind him with his claws, but it was a weak move. He'd lost a lot of blood. His vision blurred, dizziness overwhelming him. "Stay down!" a man yelled at him, but he ignored him as he once again tried to force himself back onto his knees. "Dammit, the General wanted this one alive. Someone knock him the hell out!"

He felt the needle go into his neck, and he struggled to stay awake. He had to know his daughters were free. Snarling, he rolled over and stared up at the sky, blinking rapidly to bring the bright moon above into focus as he listened to what was left of the General's soldiers as they realized their world had just been royally fucked.

"Oh, shit!"

"What?"

"They're gone!"

"What? Where the hell are they? Dammit! You better find them!"

Chase turned his head to the side, his gaze focused on the van the men were swarming around. They were gone. His babies had made it to freedom. Letting out a sigh of relief, he finally let himself go, giving into the black void that claimed him.

JADE and the twins hid beneath the van just until she was sure all attention was on Chase, and then they slipped out from under it, making their way quickly across the open ground to a forest of trees beyond. Stopping, she glanced back and watched in horror as Chase fell to the ground, then stumbled back to his feet. Her eyes were glued to him as he attacked one of the soldiers and then another. She had never seen anyone fight like him before. The overall power he wielded was breath-taking, and she couldn't look away. He was fighting for his family, for them, and it showed.

A whimper from one of the girls pulled her out of the trance she was in, and she realized they needed to get moving. Chase was trusting her to take care of the twins, and she refused to disappoint him. Nudging them gently with her nose, she pushed them away from the scene of violence and destruction. Reluctantly, they turned and scampered away.

Jade looked back one last time, freezing when she saw Chase fall to the ground, and not get back up. Fear consumed her as she watched blood begin to pool around his body. She would have run to him if one of the pups hadn't chosen that moment to whine softly. The decision was taken from her when she met Hope's light blue gaze. She would not leave them, and she could not lead them back to the General's men. They needed her. Chase had protected them, knowing full well that he would end up in the General's clutches. She would do what she knew he wanted. Her heart breaking, Jade rushed the girls out of there, leaving behind her alpha, the man she considered her second father, praying he was still alive.

14

Angel stood behind Jaxson, looking over his shoulder as his fingers flew across the keys of his laptop. He went so fast that she couldn't make sense of half of it, but he knew what he was doing, and that was all that mattered. It was early morning, and they were no closer to finding Chase and the girls than they were the night before. They were able to rule out a lot of places, but there were so many more to look at.

Her team was still there, as were some of the White River Wolves, but most had gone home to their families. The ones who remained were on Chase's special team, the one he took on missions. She'd gotten to know them better over the passing hours, and was impressed with their loyalty and dedication not only to their alpha, but to their pack as well.

When Jaxson's hands paused, then moved slowly before pausing again, Angel whispered, "Jaxson, please, give me some good news."

Jaxson sighed, running a hand through his thick, dark

blond hair, before leaning back in his chair and rubbing his tired eyes. "I have it narrowed down to two places, Angel, but the problem is, they are thousands of miles apart from each other."

"Where?" she demanded.

"One is in California, and the other in the D.C. area."

"D.C.," Steele cut in. "That's where Jinx was the last time I saw him. Jeremiah too."

Angel's eyes narrowed, "Which one do we try first?"

"I have one more I think we should look at," Becca said, tapping her monitor lightly. "The General has a place in Washington. I'm just having an issue finding the exact location. My gut is telling me that he took them there."

"Why?" Angel asked in suspicion. Why would Becca choose a place to look more closely at that Jaxson hadn't? If he'd ruled a place out, he would have a good reason, and she trusted him explicitly.

"I don't really know, to be honest," Becca admitted, "but I have learned to trust my instincts. Right now, they are screaming Washington."

"Jaxson?" Angel turned to him for confirmation.

Jaxson pulled Becca's laptop closer, then looked at her notes that she had scribbled on a tablet beside her. "I'm impressed," he said quietly. "But I want to know how you came up with some of these things. They aren't common knowledge. They can't be, or I would have found them."

"You forget," Becca replied, gritting her teeth at his mistrust, "I used to work for the bastard. I know a little bit more about how his mind works. What makes him tick. He's from Washington. That's where he grew up. It would make sense that he would go back there after you demolished the one place he felt safe in Alaska. He's hiding. But he would want to see Chase and the girls personally, to make sure they were really captured. Then he will move them."

"How the hell would you know all of that?" Phoenix snarled. "The General doesn't seem like the type who would confide in someone else, especially about his personal life."

"He didn't," she shrugged, her eyes trained on her computer, "but you all aren't the only ones with...gifts."

"You've been keeping some secrets of your own," Angel said quietly.

Becca glanced at Jaxson, then up to her. "It's safer that way," she whispered.

"We will talk about this later," Angel said, touching her lightly on the shoulder. She stiffened, but didn't pull away. Angel caught a glimpse of Becca covering a small body cowering in a corner, blood streaming down her back from the lashes of a whip, a beating she'd taken for the person she was protecting, and then there was nothing. Becca had shoved her out of her mind, and locked it down tight.

Taking a step back, Angel looked at Jaxson. "You and Becca dig deep into all three places, and find the right one. We don't have time to fly to one, just to find out we picked wrong."

"On it, boss."

There was a low buzz in the room as everyone began to talk at once, excitement beginning to build now that they were finally narrowing things down. Angel was itching to get on the road. She was so close, she could almost taste it.

Angel? Mom, can you hear me? I need you. The words

whispered through Angel's mind, so soft and distant that she almost missed them. She froze, holding up a hand for silence, and everyone in the room instantly became still.

Mom, please. Please be there.

It was Jade. The sound of her daughter's voice brought tears to her eyes. She'd tried so hard to reach both Jade and Chase since they were taken, but was unable to. There had been no answer, and she was unable to merge with them. *I'm right here, sweetheart,* she said urgently. *Talk to me, Jade. Where are you?* "Come on, baby," she said out loud, "talk to me."

I don't know for sure. The response was so faint, and she could feel Jade's exhaustion through their link. *I think I'm somewhere in Washington, near the Seattle area. The last sign I saw said North Bend, but I didn't stop. We can't stop. I have to put distance between us. I have to keep my sisters safe. I promised,* she stumbled over her words, tears evident in her voice, *I promised Chase.*

Chase isn't with you? Angel asked, already knowing the answer. If Jade promised Chase she would keep Faith and Hope safe, then he wasn't there to do it himself.

No.

It was just one word, but it spoke volumes. The pain, the total agony enveloping her daughter, made its way through the thread that held them together and into Angel, suffocating her and putting her to her knees. Nico was instantly kneeling beside her, clasping her hand tightly in his, but he did not say a word. He knew better than to interrupt when she was linked to somebody. *Is he?* She couldn't finish her question. It hurt too much, and she was unable to get the words out.

I don't know, Jade replied. *I'm so sorry, Mom. I just did what he told me to, and got the girls away. It was what he wanted.*

Angel swallowed hard, gripping Nico's hand tightly in hers. *As you should have,* she said. *You did good, baby.* She felt someone else kneel on the other side of her, and knew instantly that it was Steele. Reaching out, she covered his hand with hers, squeezing hard as she whispered to Jade, *Your dad and I are coming for you, Jade.*

I can't hold the link any longer, Jade whispered.

It's okay, baby. We're on our way. Find somewhere to hide, and I will contact you again when our plane touches down.

I'm so scared, Mom. Not for me, but for my sisters. The General can't get them.

I know, Jade, but you have to be strong. You have to keep them safe until we get there.

Mom.

Yes?

Tell Trace, she hesitated, *tell him how much I love him.*

He already knows, baby, but I will.

The link was severed before she could say more, and Jade was gone. As a shudder ran through her, she stayed quiet for a moment, fighting to get control of her emotions. Finally, she let go of Nico and Steele and rose, curling her fingers into fists, her nails digging into her palms. Glancing around the room, she said, "Jade has Faith and Hope. They've escaped. Becca was right. They are in Washington, somewhere near Seattle, close to a small town I've never heard of."

"Which one?" Jaxson asked.

"North Bend."

"And Chase?" Sable questioned, the worry evident in her voice.

"I don't know," Angel admitted. "All Jade could tell me was that he wasn't with her."

"Someone want to tell me what the hell is going on?" Trigger growled. When Angel's eyes narrowed on him, he looked around the room. "Are you all psychics or something?"

Shit. Angel had forgotten that not all members of the pack knew about the gifts she and her team possessed, along with several other members that had joined the White River Wolves in the past year. Before she could respond, Sable shook her head, "Bran or I will fill them in later. Finding Jade and the girls is more important."

"You know?"

"Yes, but I will never give up your secrets, and neither will anyone else in this room. I trust them with my life."

"Thank you," she told the woman quietly, before turning to Nico. "Call the airport and make sure the plane is ready. We leave now."

"I want to go," Bran said, stepping forward.

"Not going to happen, Bran. I need you here."

"Dammit, we have to find Chase!"

"And we will," Angel promised, "but right now I need you here. As pack beta, I'm leaving you in charge."

"I understand." Even though he agreed, she could tell he wasn't happy about it. His alpha was out there somewhere, and he was stuck in the compound, unable to help find him.

"Bran, I need you to keep Alanna and Fallon safe. The council is counting on us to watch over them, and they are now a part of our pack. Remember, above all else, we protect what is ours."

Bran bowed his head, then nodded, "Yes, Alpha."

She had never thought about what it would mean when she and Chase mated. They were both alphas, leaders, and used to being in charge. Had she thought they would go on being alphas of their own packs? Divided as they had been for a year now? She was finding out quickly that doing things the old way wasn't going to be an option. The White River Wolves now looked to her for guidance, and it would seem she and Chase would be united together, alphas to one large pack.

Angel froze, wasn't that what Chase had been trying to tell her since the very beginning? That they would be stronger together, united as one? She had done nothing but continue to deny him, thinking she needed to bring the General down so that she knew for sure her children were safe before she followed her own happiness. She had been so wrong.

"My team goes with me," she said, "but there is not enough room on the plane for everyone." She could tell the White River Wolves were not happy. Their alpha's life was on the line, and they wanted to be there, too. "I have room for two more. Slade and Sable will come with me. The rest of you are needed here. Stay vigilant and guard the pack. We have no idea what the General will do now that he doesn't have my children any longer."

"Shit," Bran muttered, "I didn't think about that. What if he retaliates?"

"Then you fight," Angel said simply.

15

Five hours later, Angel and her team were making their way stealthily to an old abandoned barn approximately two miles outside of a small town, a good two hours from Seattle. *We are here, Jade.*

Mom?

We have the building surrounded, and have cased the perimeter. There is no one here. It is safe to show yourself.

Angel watched, her heart in her throat, as a white wolf, so similar to her own, emerged from the dilapidated building, stopping to scan the area intently, before her gaze settled on Angel. *The girls won't come out. They are terrified.*

Of course, they were. They had spent their entire life as prisoners of the General, until RARE rescued them. After everything they were put through, they would be scared to death at the idea of returning to that life. *They don't have to. I'm coming to them.* Knowing there would be no holding Trace back, and that Steele would want to be near his daughter, she murmured through her comms, "Steele, Storm, and Trace, you are with me. The rest of you stay alert."

They quickly made their way to Jade, and Trace reached down and scooped her into his arms, burying his face into the soft fur at her neck. "Let's get her out of the open, Trace," Angel urged, moving past them to enter the dimly lit barn. She'd just stepped inside when there was a loud whine and then two balls of fluff came flying at her. Falling to the ground, she caught them both in her arms, holding them close, tears flowing down her cheeks. "It's okay, babies, I'm here now. Everything is going to be okay."

It was several moments before Faith shifted, and looked at her with wide, solemn eyes. "It is not okay. They killed daddy."

"What?" A pain like no other filled her, and she felt a scream of agony fighting its way up her throat. Chase was dead?

"No, Hope, we don't know that," Jade said, from where she had also shifted and was now wrapped tightly in her mate's arms, covered in a blanket.

"They shot him so many times," Faith whispered.

"Oh, God," Angel moaned, her body beginning to shake. She knew she needed to be strong, but she also knew that if Chase really was gone from this world, it would break her, and there would be no coming back from it.

She felt someone near, and then arms slipped around her. "He's alive. I know it. I feel it."

Struggling to breathe, her chest heaving as she fought

to hold the howls of rage and pain inside, Angel rasped, "You feel him? You can connect to him?" She had tried so many times, but there was always just dark nothingness.

"No," Jade admitted, "I can't. But you should have seen him, Mom. He took out most of the General's men to save us, with his hands bound in chains."

"What?" Steele asked, turning from where he stood by the door. He'd stayed back this whole time, keeping a lookout for enemies.

Angel looked up at Jade, clutching Faith and Hope tightly to her. "He was drawing their attention from you."

"I've never seen anyone fight like him," Jade said, her eyes wide with awe. "He fell down, but just got back up and went after the next one. They put bullet after bullet in him, but he didn't stop. It was like he had nothing to lose."

"No," Storm said from where she stood by her mate, "it wasn't that he had nothing to lose, Jade. There is nothing more dangerous than a man with *everything* to lose. He considers you girls his daughters, his to protect. He loves you."

Jade nodded, her emerald eyes full of tears. "He does. He told me that we are all his, even Jinx." Rubbing the wetness from her eyes, she whispered, "They took us to this place out in the middle of nowhere. There was a helicopter, and the driver said we better say our final goodbyes because we were going to be split up when we got to wherever it was they were taking us. Chase wouldn't let that happen. He told us to shift, and that I was to take care of my sisters, and get them to Mom. When I told him that I didn't want to leave him, that I was afraid we would never be able to find him, he said Angel would find him."

The howl of pain she had barely been preventing escaped; long, loud, and full of misery. Chase was out there somewhere, hurt, possibly even dying. He was counting on her to find him, and she had no idea where to start. What was she going to do? Her mate needed her, and she didn't know where to turn.

16

"He's a stubborn bastard, and strong as hell," Chase heard someone mutter.

"Is he going to make it?" The voice was low and emotionless.

"It is too soon to tell, General. I will do my best, but I am a scientist, not a doctor." General. The fucking General was there. The bastard who wanted to take everything he loved from him. Chase moved his hands experimentally, and then his arms, not enough to attract attention, but just enough to tell he was not bound down. They thought he was hurt so badly that he was incapacitated. That was their first mistake.

"I suggest you do better than that," the General commanded darkly, "if you want to live, that is."

"Yes, sir." The quiver in his voice almost made Chase feel sorry for the guy…almost. What stopped him was the way the man was brutally removing the bullets from his body. Digging around in Chase's flesh as if he didn't care if it hurt or not. He was not someone to feel compassion for, as the feeling was not mutual.

Chase opened his eyes just a crack, peeking through narrow slits to look at the men who stood over him. The one digging into his shoulder was short, scrawny, and a thin layer of sweat dotted his brow. He reached up to wipe it away, and then went back to mutilating Chase's shoulder. It fucking burned where the scalpel sliced into his skin, but Chase stayed silent. He refused to give them the satisfaction of seeing him suffer.

The other man was bigger, and he knew immediately it was the one they called the General, but he was not as large as Chase had imagined him. However, there was no doubt in his mind that he was the one he needed to watch. He gave off a feeling of power, and Chase could tell he would be a force to be reckoned with, but he wasn't afraid. The General had threatened his family, kidnapped his children, and was the reason Chase had spent months alone, without the woman he loved more than life itself. No, he was a lot of things, but afraid wasn't one of them.

"I severely underestimated you, Chase Montgomery," the General said, taking a step closer to where Chase lay. "I will not make that mistake again."

You just did, Chase thought, feeling his fangs drop and his claws shoot out his fingertips as he partially shifted. Rising quickly, he ignored the sudden dizziness that swamped him, and pushed himself off the cold metal exam table. He let out a roar of fury as he sank his teeth into the scientist's neck and sliced at the General's jugular with a claw. The General moved just in time, evading the killing blow, but screaming as Chase's claw sliced his cheek wide open, catching his eye as well. Chase felt a sharp sting in the side of his neck, and another in his arm, as he dropped the dead scientist to the floor and staggered forward, taking another swipe at the General.

"Son of a bitch," the General yelled, grabbing his arm where a piece of flesh now hung from it. "Someone stop him!"

Chase felt two more tranquilizer darts enter his body, and he snarled as he struggled forward on leaden feet for one last try. The General had made his life hell for so long, the bastard deserved to pay. Baring his teeth, he fell forward just as he was tackled from behind, and landed on the General. He sank his teeth deep into the man's shoulder, grinning in satisfaction at the sound of the General's screams. "Get him off me! Get him the hell away from me!"

Chase bit down harder, refusing to let go, even as he felt two more darts pierce his skin. It might be enough to kill him, but all Chase could think about was ending his mate's misery. She didn't deserve the hell she had been put through. Neither did his children. The drugs were working their way through his system, his entire body becoming numb, but he still didn't let go. The General hit him over and over in the head with his good fist, but Chase wouldn't budge. He'd taken his babies! And he still had Jinx under his control. Chase had to get him out of there. He needed to be home with his family, not doing the General's bidding.

Two of the soldiers grabbed Chase by his arms, trying to pull him off. He growled, locking his hands around the General's throat and squeezing. He shook his head, trying to get rid of the fogginess, reveling in the scream that tore from the General's lips when his fangs dug even deeper.

Who are you? Chase wasn't psychic, but hearing the voice in his mind was nothing new to him. He'd spoken to Angel this way, along with others. Nothing surprised him anymore. *Why are you trying to save me?*

Chase paused, struggling to clear his head so that he could finish what he started. The drugs were so far in his system now, that he knew it wouldn't be long before he passed out. *Dammit, who are you?* The voice demanded again, louder this time.

The General's screams had stopped now, and he lay beneath Chase unmoving. But his heart still beat. Chase could feel it. Snarling again, he tried to finish it, to kill the bastard who had hurt his family, but the darkness was coming for him, and he was unable to fight it any longer. *I've failed you this time, son,* he whispered, *but it won't happen again. This isn't the end. We will leave this place together. I will bring you home. I promise.*

Son? He heard the confusion in the man's voice. *Home?*

Chase could not respond, and he closed his eyes as he felt Jinx enter his mind impatiently, trying to get his answers his own way. The last thing he heard was Jinx's loud curse as he succumbed to the darkness.

JINX SLAMMED his fist into the wall of his hotel room, watching in satisfaction as a small section of the drywall crumbled to the floor, before swinging around and stalking over to the bed to sit on the end of it. Resting his elbows on his knees, he lowered his head and shoved his hands into his dark hair, clutching it in his fists. How the hell had the General captured Chase Montgomery, the alpha of the White River Wolves? Hell, the man was his mother's mate. He'd seen brief glimpses in Chase's mind before he passed out, images of him with his jaws wrapped tightly around the General's shoulder, and blood flowing everywhere. There was so much of it, and he couldn't tell what was from Chase and what belonged to the General. What was clear in the alpha's mind though, was that he did what he did for one reason only, his family. And that family included Jinx. The man claimed Jinx as his son, even though he had never met him, and he would give his life for him. Jade had tried to tell him that Chase felt that way about him, but he hadn't believed her. What kind of man would want to claim someone like him as a son? His own father didn't have a choice, but Chase? Jinx swallowed hard, clenching his hands tightly into fists. Chase was unlike any other person Jinx had ever met.

Jinx rose and began pacing the small room swiftly, trying to decide what to do. He was closer to the White River Wolves compound than D.C., where he was sure they held Chase. He needed to warn Angel, in case she didn't already know what was going on. But he didn't have time to go to Colorado. He had to get to D.C. quickly, because if Chase hadn't managed to kill the General, which Jinx didn't think he had, then his life was on the line. Before the General would have been content to watch him suffer while being tortured on a daily basis, now he would want Chase dead.

Stopping in front of a wall, Jinx leaned forward and placed his palms against the smooth surface, closing his eyes and concentrating. Very carefully, he slipped inside the General's mind delving further and further until he found what he was looking for beyond the blank stillness he initially encountered. There it was, the faint beat of the bastard's heart. He lived.

Cursing, Jinx changed direction and reached out for the one person he had never fully connected with, his eyes widening at the deep misery and utter loss he instantly felt. *Angel?* When there was no response, he tried again, *Angel, it's Jinx.*

There was silence for a moment and then, *Jinx?*

He heard her shock, felt it, along with the overwhelming pain, which meant she had to know that Chase was missing. *I just connected with Chase,* he told her. *He needs help, Angel. I'm on my way to D.C., but you need to get there fast. He might not last much longer.*

Oh, my God. He's alive? He sensed her relief, but then the fear took over. *You are sure he's in D.C.? We have been trying to find him ever since we rescued your sisters this morning.*

Rescued his sisters? *What the hell are you talking about?* he bit out. The General had sent him to California on a mission, which meant he was there as an assassin because that was what all of his missions entailed. It had taken him longer to complete this one because there were three different targets, and he had just wrapped it up a couple of hours ago. He'd planned on staying over one more night before he went back to D.C., until he had connected with Chase.

The General kidnapped Chase and your sisters, Jinx. All of them.

All of them? His brow furrowed in confusion. As far as he knew, Jade was his only sister.

Jade, Hope, and Faith.

Hope and Faith, the two little girls Angel had rescued

the year before who now lived with Chase. His sisters. *What the fuck?* he snarled, dark, furious anger closing in on him.

They managed to get away because, Angel stopped for a second, and he could hear the hitch in her breath before she continued, *because Chase attacked the General's soldiers, drawing all of their attention to him. He was shot several times, and the girls didn't know if he made it.*

He made it, Jinx growled, pushing off from the wall and resuming his pacing around the room. *But then he attacked the General, almost killing him, so we need to get to D.C. now.*

He attacked the General? she asked incredulously. *Why would he do that on his own?*

Jinx stopped, bowing his head and swearing darkly. *He wanted to kill him for hurting his family,* he rasped. *He wanted me to be free. He wanted to bring me home.* The last was barely a whisper. He still could not believe someone could care for him, after everything he had done, like Chase did. Before he could stop himself he asked, *Why would he want to bring me there? After everything I have done?*

Everything you were forced to do, Jinx, Angel growled. *You have no choice. You do those things to protect your family, and Chase would do the same if he was in your position. Any of us would. He understands.*

He thinks of me as his son.

He heard the pride in her voice when she replied, *He always has. Since the moment he found out about you and Jade, you were his. He knows Steele is your father, but he still claims you.*

He is willing to die for me.

Yes, Angel agreed softly, *he is.*

Jinx turned and stalked over to the door, opening it

and not bothering to stop to see if it shut behind him. *I'm on my way to D.C. Right now, the General lives, but Chase got him good. He may not make it.*

Tell me where to meet you.

Contact me when you get to D.C., Jinx told her as he pushed the front doors of the hotel open wide, walking out into the bright sun. *Angel?*

Yes.

I will keep him alive. He couldn't promise more than that. He had no idea what he was going to be walking into when he got back. But no matter what, he wasn't letting Chase Montgomery die.

17

Angel held Hope close, whispering softly to her as she gently stroked a hand lovingly down the soft fur on her back. Hope refused to shift back, feeling safer in wolf form, and Angel wasn't going to push her. She sat on the couch in Chase's living room, surrounded by her children, her team, and her pack…her family. They had returned to the White River Wolves compound less than a half an hour ago, and Angel was getting ready to leave again soon. As much as she wanted to stay a little while longer with her children, the need to get to D.C. and find Chase was driving at her. It had been over an hour since Jinx contacted her, and she could not wait any longer.

"I need to go," she murmured, leaning down to kiss Faith's cheek and then bury her face in Hope's fur. At Faith's protest, Angel slipped her arm around her waist and pulled her closer. "I have to, sweetie. I'm going to get your daddy and bring him home."

"I'm scared," Faith whispered, pressing into Angel's side. "What if that bad woman comes back?"

"She won't be able to get to you," Angel promised softly.

"She won't?"

"I'm leaving some very special people here to watch over you and your sisters, Faith. They won't let any bad people get near you."

Faith looked up at her, her big eyes wary, "Who?" she demanded, and Angel had to hide her smile. The child sounded just like her. It warmed her heart.

"Trace and Jade will be here, along with Steele and Storm," Angel told her.

"Angel," Storm cut in, "we want to help you get your mate back."

"I know you do," Angel told her, "but I am trusting you with the rest of my heart."

Storm nodded, understanding dawning in her gaze. Angel needed to know her children were well-protected, because there was every chance that the General could have already sent his men after the girls again.

"We won't let you down," Steele promised, standing close to his mate. "We will guard the twins as if they were our own."

Angel inhaled deeply, snuggling the twins closer before she continued. "Phoenix, Bane, and Ryker, you are staying here, too."

"Fuck that," Phoenix snarled. "I'm not letting you go against the General without me there!"

"Phoenix," Angel paused, looking down at the girls. They were both exhausted, struggling to keep their eyes open, and this was a conversation they did not need to be a part of. Giving them both one last hug and kiss, she motioned to Jade, "Can you and Trace please take the girls upstairs? They need to rest."

"Angel, I should be going with you," Trace said quietly, indecision warring in his eyes.

"No, Trace, you should be here, taking care of my daughters."

"But you will need more than one sniper."

"I have two," Angel told him. "Sapphire and Charlotte."

There was a soft gasp of surprise, and Angel knew it came from Charlotte. She hadn't been around the woman very much, but if Chase trusted her, then she would, too.

Trace turned a hard gaze in Charlotte's direction. "Are you good?" he growled.

"She's the best," Bran stated. "She doesn't miss."

Trace's eyes never left Charlotte's. "That true?"

Charlotte's chin lifted, and she glared at him defiantly, "Yes, but if you need proof, I'd be happy to take you out back and show you." The word asshole was left off, but Angel suppressed a smile when she read it in Charlotte's mind. She knew Trace heard it too, because Charlotte wasn't used to being around people like her team. Her thoughts and emotions were loud and clear, as was the fact that she wasn't going to let Trace talk to her as if she was a piece of shit.

Trace stared at her for a long moment before reaching down and gathering a now-sleeping Faith in his arms. "Not necessary."

When Jade picked up Hope, Angel stood and pulled them both into her arms. "I love you, Jade," she murmured. "Stay safe."

A tear escaped, as Jade whispered, "I love you too, Mom. Bring Chase home. We need him." It was the first time Jade had told her that she loved her, and she really needed to hear that right now.

Angel's heart hurt as she replied, "Yes, we do."

She watched Trace lead her daughters up the stairs, followed closely by Steele and Storm. She knew they would be safe, no matter what the General threw their way, but they weren't the only enforcements she was leaving behind. Once they were out of sight, she turned back to the men and women who filled the large living room. "We obviously can't all go," she started, and when Phoenix began to protest, along with several others, she held up a hand for silence. "The people in this compound need enforcers to keep them safe. My daughters need protection. We don't know if the General sent someone after them before Chase incapacitated him or not. We cannot all go and leave them vulnerable for attack. It just isn't going to happen. From now, until we are home with Chase, this place is on lockdown."

There was murmuring and then Bran said, "The pack isn't going to like that, Angel."

"Would they rather be dead?" Angel asked, raising an eyebrow. "Because that is the other option if there are assassins out there gunning for us."

"Shit," Slade growled, raking a hand through his hair. "You're right. We need to keep everyone safe, which means no one leaves the compound and we step up our security. I'll handle it." Slade was the White River Wolves head enforcer, and from what Angel knew, he was damn good at his job.

"Agreed," she said, before glancing slowly around at all of the people in the room. "This is the way it is going to be, whether you like it or not. I am your acting alpha right now, and you will do as I say. Understood?" When there was a murmur of agreement in the room, she continued, "Phoenix, I need you here for two reasons."

"They better be fucking good," he snarled.

"Serenity and your unborn baby." When Phoenix swore loudly, she said, "You know as well as I do that the General wants them, Phoenix. We cannot let that happen. You need to be here to keep them safe, because no one can protect them better than you." Phoenix hesitated, but finally nodded in agreement. "Ryker, I'm leaving you here as well. You and River are in charge of keeping Alanna and Fallon safe. I cannot stress enough how important that sweet bear is going to be to this pack. Do you understand?"

"Yes, Alpha."

"Bane, I need you to be a ghost." She did not elaborate. He would know exactly what she meant. It was up to him to move around in the compound, unseen, watching for any hidden danger.

"Done," Bane said with a quick nod. The man was short on words, but she had come to realize quickly over the past few weeks that he was honorable and when the stakes were down, he was one you wanted on your side. His life had changed drastically when the General murdered everyone in their village to show his brother, Steele, a lesson. He'd had to change who he was, becoming stronger and more aggressive. She knew it wasn't who he was deep down, but it was who he was forced to be now.

"Nico."

Before she could finish, he interjected, "I'm going." She just nodded, because she had known it would be his response, and he would not back down. He was her second in command, and he did not take that lightly.

"I will look out for your family," Phoenix promised.

As the two men bumped fists, Angel's gaze went to the pack beta. "Sapphire, Jaxson, and Flame are with me." When the low rumble began in Bran's chest, Angel said, "I need her, Bran."

"You are sending my mate right back into hell!" he roared. "What if they capture her again?"

"They won't," Angel promised, reaching out to place a hand on Flame's arm when she would have spoken up. "I won't allow it."

"I can take care of myself," Flame snapped, her eyes flashing in anger.

Bran bared his teeth, a low growl escaping. "You've made that perfectly clear, princess," he snarled, turning to leave the room.

"Bran," Angel called out, waiting until he stopped, but did not turn around. She knew he was close to shifting, and was leaving so that he didn't hurt anyone in his anger, but she had learned so much in the past few days, and couldn't let him go without saying, "I promise you, I will bring your mate home."

She heard the gasp of surprise from Flame, and saw Bran incline his head slightly. "Thank you, Alpha," he said, before leaving the house.

"Angel, why would you promise him something like that?" Flame demanded. "He doesn't own me!"

Angel turned toward her, gently squeezing the arm she still held. "Because, Flame, I now know what it is like to have your mate out there in danger, their life hanging in the balance, while you have no fucking clue what's going on. It hurts, Flame, so much. The pain is excruciating, the fear like nothing I have ever felt before, and I never want to have someone else feel what I am feeling right now if I can prevent it."

Not giving Flame a chance to respond, preferring to let her words have time to sink in, Angel stepped back and ordered, "The rest of you will remain here and keep this compound safe." There was a chorus of "Yes, Alpha," even though she knew they all wanted to go with her. Hell, she would take them if she could, every last one of them. She could use all the help she could get when she went up against the General's soldiers. Unfortunately, they just did not have room on the plane. They would need empty seats to bring Chase, and hopefully Jinx, home.

Not willing to waste any more time, Angel turned and walked to the door. Glancing back, she said, "Let's go get Chase."

18

Chase groaned, pain swamping him as he struggled to pry his eyes open. Thoughts and images raced through his head as he slowly became aware of his surroundings. His chest was on fire, and his arms felt as if they were being wrenched from his body. There wasn't an area on him that didn't hurt, but it was worth it. If his memory served him correctly, the General was fighting his own battle right now, unless he'd already lost it. Could they be that lucky? Could he have killed the sadistic son of a bitch?

Finally managing to open his eyes just enough to peer out into the dimness in front of him, he looked around in confusion, shaking his head to try and clear the fogginess from his mind so he could focus. No wonder his arms hurt like a bitch. He was in a large cage of some sort surrounded by thick, steel bars, empty as far as he could tell, except for him. His vision was blurry, but he did not sense anyone near him. He hung from the ceiling by silver chains wrapped tightly around each wrist, arms spread wide, naked except for a pair of jogging pants that had definitely seen better days. His bare feet just touched the ground, and he tried to place them firmly on the cold cement to relieve the pressure in his arms, but he was almost too weak to hold himself up. Did they think this was going to stop him? They had kidnapped his children, hurt his mate, and infiltrated his compound, placing his entire pack in danger. Grasping the chains tightly in his hands, he gritted his teeth in determination, closing his eyes and summoning the power within him. The power that came with being alpha, the power that gave him more strength and will to fight than most, because he had something to fight for. They would not hurt the people he loved again.

"Chase?" the voice was soft and urgent, the scent of fear radiating around him. "Chase, I'm going to get you out of here. I don't know how, but I will. I promise."

Who the hell was it? He knew her scent, had smelled it before. He knew that voice, so low and timid. Where had he seen her, talked to her? Her voice came from behind him and off to the left. He tried to turn to see who she was, but it was impossible.

"Stop," she whispered. "You'll bring attention to us."

"There's no one here," he spit out angrily.

"No, but they are always watching."

Raising his head, Chase glanced slowly around what he could see of the dimly lit area. Squinting through blearing eyes, he saw he was in what looked like one huge room. Maybe an abandoned factory or warehouse, he wasn't sure. There were more cages across from him, but they were all empty, as was the rest of the area. "Who are you?" he asked, lowering his gaze to the floor once more as he drew more power to him, gaining enough strength to stand without the aid of the chains. When she didn't respond right away, he growled, "Tell me, dammit."

There was silence, and then she hesitantly whispered, "It's me, Mr. Montgomery. Amber."

"Amber?" It took him a moment, but then it all came back to him. Amber was the scientist RARE brought back with them from Alaska. The girl had been scared of her own shadow, but had somehow managed to help save Steele and Storm from the General. But, what was she doing with him again? "Did they find you?" He knew Angel had been worried that they would track the girl down and either capture or kill her. He'd offered her a place to stay, but she'd insisted on going home to her sister. When she remained quiet, he said, "Amber, talk to me."

Finally she murmured, "No, they didn't find me. I came back willingly."

That made no sense. Why would anyone come back to this hell unless, "Does the General have your sister, Amber? Is that why you are here?"

Before she could answer, there was a loud bang as a door was flung open at the other end of the building and someone stepped inside, immediately followed by two others. Amber let out a small squeak of surprise, and then there was nothing.

Chase stared at the floor, feeling the low thrum of power coursing through his body. He kept quiet, waiting to see what would happen. It didn't take long for the men to cross the room, and Chase's nostrils flared when he inhaled a scent that he had never come across before, but one that bore a resemblance to that of his mate. Jinx had arrived.

"The General isn't here," one of the men said, stalking over to the cage and glaring inside.

"Where is he?" That was definitely Jinx. He would remember his voice anywhere, the one he'd heard in his mind right after attacking the General.

"Like you don't know," came the sarcastic reply.

"If I knew, I wouldn't have asked," was the cold response.

"Shut the fuck up, Denny," the other man grunted. "The General is out of commission for the time being."

"Out of commission? What the fuck is that supposed to mean?" Jinx ground out. "And who's this sorry bastard?"

Denny chuckled, opening the cage and stepping inside. "He's the reason the General is lying in a bed, fighting for his life right now."

Come a little closer, Chase thought, *and you will be in one next to him.*

A low chuckle sounded in his mind, and then *Let me find out what's going on with the General before you take him out. I need to figure out if...*Jinx was suddenly quiet before he growled, *who's here with you?*

Stand down, Jinx, Chase growled, keeping his head lowered so that he didn't attract more attention. He knew with all of the power flowing through his body right now that his eyes would have gone wolf and would be glowing a bright blue. *She's a friend.*

Your friend smells like the General, Jinx snarled.

Chase stiffened, inhaling deeply. He caught the scent of Jinx, the filthy soldier standing in front of him, the other man, and Amber. Sorting the different smells out in his mind, he concentrated just on the young woman, and had to bite back the growl that threatened to break free. Jinx was right, she shared the General's scent. She might have been around him recently, but it was more than that. It was something ingrained in her. She was somehow related to the General. Chase felt his fangs lengthen, anger seeping through him at the thought of being played by her. She had been in his damn compound, near his family! They had all fallen for her story about taking a job to help save money for her sister. They'd trusted her, and she had deceived them.

No! It wasn't like that. Amber's words flowed through his mind, filled with panic and something else. Remorse? *I never meant to hurt anyone. Not ever. I can't help who my father is.* His head snapped up at that, a roar ripping from his throat. Denny was the unlucky one who was close enough to feel his wrath. Clasping the chains tightly, Chase pulled himself up and struck out with his legs, wrapping them around Denny's waist and yanking him close. Not thinking twice, he leaned down and bit into the man's jugular, twisting hard, and tearing the skin at his neck open. Spitting out blood, he dropped the lifeless body to the ground and glared at Jinx and the other soldier. Jinx was dressed all in black, with short brown hair, and dark brown eyes. He had a gun strapped to his hip, another on his thigh, and Chase could see the handles of several knives hidden in different places of his cargo pants. And was that a sword on his back?

"Holy shit," the soldier said in awe, staring down at where Denny now lay on the ground, blood flowing from him. "How did you do that? We pumped you with so many drugs when you took out the General, that you shouldn't even be moving right now!"

Chase, you have to stop. They will kill you! Please, stop.

Chase bared his teeth, breathing through the burning agony in his shoulder as he began to pull hard on the chains that held him.

Chase, please. I can't let you die, but if I have to show myself, it will ruin all of the good I'm trying to do here.

Good? You are the devil's daughter!

He heard the pain and acceptance in her voice when she replied, *Yes, I am. But, Chase, I am not him. I do what I can to help the people he tries to hurt. Just like I helped Steele and Storm. But I can't do that if he finds out what I've been doing. He will lock me in a cell and throw away the key. He doesn't care who I am, Chase. I am nobody to him, but I am somebody to every single person I save.* There was a pause, and then she whispered, *Please, don't take that from me. It is all that I have.*

Chase heard a loud commotion at the door, and then it burst open, two soldiers rushing in. "What the hell is going on in here?" one of them demanded.

"Seems like your guy got a little too close to the big bad wolf," Jinx drawled, stepping into the cage and picking up what was left of Denny to throw him out.

Aware that all eyes were on him, inquiring and calculating, Chase snarled, "You want to be next?'

Jinx turned back, his eyes trained on him, even as Chase felt the slight movement behind him. *Don't,* he cautioned, *she's not what she seems.*

I know, was all Jinx said before stepping up close to him. "I heard you challenged the General," he growled, "which means you've got balls. But trust me, wolf, you don't want to fuck with me."

Chase bared his teeth, making a show of yanking on the chains again. "I'm no more afraid of you than I was of him."

"That's your first mistake," Jinx said coldly, and Chase knew that if things were different, he would be dead right now. Jinx was not one to mess around. If he felt threatened, he eliminated the problem. It was what he was trained to do, and Chase did not fault him for it.

Before he could respond, the door opened and a dark, imposing figure entered, flanked by two others. He was large and foreboding, and walked with an edge of power that immediately captured Chase's attention.

The man walked toward them, stopping in front of the cage. Chase snarled at him, unwilling to back down. The bastard just looked at him, raising an eyebrow. "Someone want to explain to me what the hell is going on here?" he commanded. When no one responded, he looked at Jinx. "I asked a question."

Jinx turned to glare at him, his hands hanging loosely at his sides as he growled, "I don't answer to you."

The man let out a short laugh, "Actually, with the General incapacitated at the moment, you do. Now I will ask again, what is going on here?" Jinx returned the man's glare, but refused to answer. "You obviously don't know who I am, son."

"I obviously don't give a shit."

The man threw back his head and laughed, and then with an evil half grin, he motioned to one of his men. The guy didn't make it very far. He made the mistake of reaching for Jinx, and was on the ground, knocked out cold, a second later.

"And don't call me son," Jinx snarled. "There are only two men in this world who have earned the right to call me that, and you aren't one of them." Walking out of the cage, Jinx slammed the door shut behind him, scowling at the newcomer before stalking across the floor away from everyone.

Just before he reached the door, the man hollered, "My name is Jerome Livingston." Chase saw Jinx pause, as if the name meant something to him. "You can call me Sir or Boss. Until the General gets better, if he does, you will answer to me, whether you want to or not. If you don't, you will die, simple as that."

Chase felt a low growl of rage begin to rise in his chest, but shoved it back down hard. That would be the first, and the last time Jerome Livingston threatened Jinx. Once he figured out how to get out of the chains binding him, the bastard was a dead man.

Jinx walked out of the building without looking back, which was a huge blow to Jerome's pride. "Pick that dumb son of a bitch up and let's get out of here. I have things to take care of," he snapped. With one last glance at Chase, he shook his head. "Don't think I don't know who you are, Chase Montgomery of the White River Wolves. Not only do I know who you are, but I know that you are the reason one of our top men is in surgery as we speak. But don't worry, I have it on very good authority that he *will* make it. I think I will keep you around so that he can kill you himself later."

Jerome left, the rest of the soldiers following close

behind. When they were gone, Chase let out a sigh of relief. He'd been worried that one of them would discover Amber, and as angry as he was at her for lying to them all, he did not want her dead. "Amber," he muttered, "you better get the hell out of here before someone comes back." When there was no answer, he tried again, "Amber, you seriously need to go." When there was still no response, he closed his eyes and concentrated, inhaling deeply. Her scent was in the air, but not as strong as before. It was slowly ebbing away. She was gone. So much for his rescue party.

19

"Dammit," Angel spat, throwing her knife into the ground. Frustration filled her as she waited impatiently for Jinx to contact her. They had arrived in D.C. the day before, and when she was unable to reach her son, they found a place on the edge of the city to stay at until they heard from him.

Angel was out behind the hotel, sitting on a log within a small cluster of trees. The cool, crisp air and music from the birds in the branches above should have helped calm her, but nothing was working. She had tried several times to merge with Chase, but was still unable to. She felt lost and empty without him near, and a part of her was terrified he had already left this world, even though she knew in her heart that he still lived. She was unused to dealing with all of the emotions that bombarded her lately, and they pissed her off. She was not a weak person. She couldn't afford to be.

"Nothing?"

Sable's voice interrupted Angel's thoughts, and it

pissed her off even more that she hadn't heard the woman's approach. "If I had something, I sure as hell wouldn't be sitting here."

She instantly regretted her snide remark, but wasn't surprised at Sable's sassy reply. "Then maybe you should get off your ass and find something. While Chase is out there, going through who knows what, we are stuck here, and I for one, am tired of waiting."

Angel removed her knife from the ground, and then slowly raised her eyes to meet Sable's dark ones. Instead of reprimanding her, Angel asked softly, "What's your story, Sable?"

"What do you mean?" Sable hedged.

"You are a good enforcer, loyal to a fault. You aren't afraid to stand up for what you believe in, nor are you afraid of dying for those you care about. You would give your life in a heartbeat for Chase, and not just because he is your alpha." Sable stiffened, but did not respond. "I have looked into you, Sable." When a low growl escaped, Angel held up a hand. "It was nothing personal. I investigated everyone in the pack when Lily was taken, but some I have followed more closely than others since then."

"Why me?"

"Because you intrigue me," Angel admitted, letting a small smile show.

Sable lifted her chin, defiance in her gaze, "And what have you learned?"

"You grew up in the pack," Angel started, slipping her knife back into the sheath at her ankle. "You have a loving family, with three very protective older brothers, all of which have mated and are now living with their mates' packs in different states. You used to be an elementary school teacher in town, and you loved it, but you quit suddenly six years ago. You have been an enforcer for Chase for the past five years, which drives your brothers crazy. Do you want me to go on?"

Sable shrugged, "Whatever."

Angel stood, closing the distance between them and laying a hand gently on Sable's arm. "I know a lot more, Sable," she said softly, hating the way the woman trembled in agitation and fear now. "I'm sorry. I hate that I violated your privacy the way that I did. I shouldn't have brought it up."

"Then why did you?" Tears filled Sable's eyes, and she turned to look out into the trees surrounding them.

"Because I want you to know, that no matter what, you can always count on me, Sable. I will always be here for you, just like Chase is."

Sable bit her bottom lip, still refusing to look in Angel's direction. "Chase saved me," she whispered. "He gave me purpose, something to live for. He was there for me when I needed someone."

"And now he needs you."

Sable jerked her arm from Angel's grasp and turned quickly, her gun raised and trained on the man who stood in front of them. "Who are you?"

"It is okay, Sable," Angel interjected, reaching out to try and push the gun down. "He's my son."

Sable's eyes narrowed, her gaze never leaving Jinx, as she refused to lower her weapon. "Talk," she growled.

Angel saw a look of admiration cross Jinx's face before he nodded. "Chase is being held at a facility about an hour from here. It took me a while to find him because it is a different place than the General normally takes them."

"Them?" Sable asked.

"Them. His victims. His prey. The people he wants to fuck with," Jinx said.

"You're an ass," Sable snarled. Angel wanted to laugh at the exchange, but was too worried about Chase. She was conscious of the rest of her team arriving, placing themselves strategically around her and Sable.

Jinx grinned, but then sobered quickly as he glanced at all of them before continuing, "We have a problem. My plan was to slip him out and make it look like he escaped, but I can't. I am being watched too closely. If I make a move, they will know and my position will be compromised."

"Fuck your position," Sable snarled. "Chase's life is more important."

"And what about my life?" Jinx growled, his dark brown eyes flashing emerald briefly, and then back to their normal color. Angel gasped, having never seen them do anything like that before. "The General is in bed, recovering from his fight with Chase. A new boss has been brought in to take over until he can lead again."

"Who?" Jaxson interrupted.

"His name is Jerome Livingston."

"I've never heard of him," Angel said.

"He is very powerful," Jinx told them. "And he has a lot of backing behind him. He will kill you without thinking twice, and his eyes are on my every little move right now."

"What if he follows you here?" Sapphire asked, taking a step closer to Jinx. Her eyes were full of worry, and love for a nephew she had never met.

Jinx looked at her, his brow furrowing in confusion as he drew in her scent. "Who are you?"

Sapphire smiled tremulously, as she whispered, "I'm your father's sister."

"My father's family is dead."

"No," Sapphire said, taking another step closer. "Everyone thought we were, even the General, but Bane and I survived. Storm found us, and we now fight alongside RARE to rid this world of the General."

"That's far enough," Jinx growled, stopping Sapphire when she would have come closer to him. "I don't do hugs and kisses, or any of that mushy shit."

"You really are an ass," Sable muttered.

"No," Angel said quietly, "he's not. He just wasn't raised to show his emotions."

"She's right, I was raised to kill, nothing more," Jinx ground out. Angel felt the sadness in his words, even though she knew the others could not. She knew her son only killed to protect the people he cared about. He didn't enjoy it. "To answer your question, a couple of Jerome's puppets did follow me. They are taking a small nap right now, which means we need to hurry this conversation along so that I can get back to them."

"Where is the facility?" Angel asked, knowing it was futile to try and convince Jinx how much he needed his family right now. He was a lone wolf, and even though he may be asking for help to save Chase's life, he would never ask anyone to help save his own.

For the next ten minutes, Jinx gave them directions on how to get to the old warehouse where Chase was being held, along with a detailed layout of the place. "He is chained up in a cage, starved and beaten every couple of hours." He hesitated, "I haven't been able to help him myself, but Amber has."

"Amber?" Angel only knew of one Amber, but it couldn't be her, could it? "What does she look like?"

Jinx sighed, glancing up at the darkening skies. "She is the same one."

"Dammit, I told her she needed to stay with the White River Wolves. I knew the General would find her again."

"It's not what you think," Jinx told her.

"Then what the hell is it? That girl is too naive to be caught up in this hell."

Jinx let out a rough, low laugh. "Yeah, all sweet and innocence that one."

"Jinx."

"She is the General's daughter," he told her.

"Oh, my God," Charlotte whispered. "Amber? She was so nice."

"Unfortunately, for her, she really is that nice," Jinx replied, "and it is going to get her ass killed."

"You care about her," Angel said, still reeling from the fact that the woman who had helped Steele and Storm escape their prison in Alaska just weeks before was related to the evil bastard they all wanted to bring down.

"She's a good person. She doesn't deserve the life that was handed to her."

"I thought you didn't do all of that mushy bullshit," Sable murmured.

Jinx's eyes snapped to hers. "I reserve it for certain people. Like the ones who have put their own lives on the line time after time to save others."

"She is the reason your father made it out alive in Alaska," Angel told Jinx. "She saved both him and Storm."

Jinx's eyes hardened, once again flashing a dark green before returning to their normal color, and she watched as his hands curled into fists, "She is nothing like the General. Nothing."

"We will bring her home with us, Jinx," Angel promised.

"She won't go," was all Jinx said before turning away from them. "I need to leave. You have to get Chase out of there tonight, Angel. He is strong, stronger than almost anyone I know, but no one can endure what he is right now for any length. I will do what I can to help." With those last words, he was gone.

20

"Chase. Chase, you have to wake up."

Chase groaned, trying to lift his head to look at the female who stood in front of him, but he couldn't seem to get his body to cooperate. "Amber," he mumbled her name, through dry, chapped lips.

"Yes, it's me. I'm going to get you out of here, Chase."

He tried to pull away from her, shaking his head as best he could. "You have to leave. They will find you."

"No, *we* have to leave."

"You said they are always watching," he muttered, a sharp pain slicing up through the back of his head.

"Normally, that is true," she agreed, "but I slipped something into the guard's drink who is on surveillance duty, so right now he's sleeping. There are two other guards outside, but I darted them both, so they should be out for a while, too. All of the others are at the main facility."

Chase felt the chains on his arms begin to loosen, and then suddenly they were gone as they clattered loudly to the floor. He almost followed them down, until Amber slid her arm around his waist and held on tightly, somehow bearing most of his weight.

"Oh, no!" she grunted, her hand tightening on his side, "we need to go now!"

Chase struggled to stay on his feet, concentrating on moving one foot in front of the other. It was a slow process, but they made it out of the cage and across the room to the front door. Amber was panting hard as she opened the door, helping him through it, and letting it slam shut behind them. "They will kill you," he rasped, worry filling him for the young woman. He had thought she'd left him after her first visit, but she ended up coming back numerous times, talking to him, and even slipping into the cage a couple of times to give him water when no one was around. He'd worried about the cameras then too, but she'd told him she had taken care of it.

"Then I will die knowing I helped save an important man," she replied, looking around again before motioning to the right. "Let's go."

"How the hell did the General father a child like you? So selfless and caring?"

"I think God gave me to him as a joke," Amber huffed wryly, almost staggering beneath his weight. "I will have to ask him if I ever make it to Heaven someday."

"You will make it," Chase promised, breathing harshly as he tried to tune out the violent pain racking his body. "God accepts all angels, as do the spirits."

Amber stopped, looking up at him with wide eyes. He realized she was letting him catch his breath, when she teased, "You didn't think I was such an angel when you found out who I was. You called me the devil's daughter, I believe."

Chase squinted down at the vision before him through blurry eyes. She was beautiful, seriously an angel, and did not even realize it. "I was wrong, Amber," he said harshly.

"No, you weren't," she whispered, tightening her grip on him as they began to move slowly through the forest of trees surrounding the large building they had just left. "The General is the devil."

"Yes," Chase agreed, "but I am starting to second guess whether or not you really are his daughter."

"Like I could get so lucky," Amber replied.

"What do we have here?"

Chase froze when he heard Jerome Livingston's voice. The man had visited him several times, beating him viciously each time. He was a mean mother, and made sure everyone knew it, especially Jinx. For some reason, Jerome seemed to have it out for him. It was as if he were just waiting for Jinx to mess up so that he could turn his fists onto him. Chase always made sure that never happened though. He was careful to keep Jerome's full attention on him the times Jinx was in the room with them. He didn't know if Jerome knew that there was a connection between him and Jinx. If he did, then he was pushing to see if Jinx gave a shit. Chase made sure that it looked like he didn't.

"Did you really think we would let you get away so easily?"

Chase heard Amber's swift intake of breath as Jerome appeared in front of them, a woman with long black hair and dark brown eyes at his side. "Hello, sister."

He felt Amber tense, as she replied, "Ebony. I didn't know you were back."

"Of course, you didn't," Ebony scoffed, "or you never would have done something so stupid."

Jerome placed a hand in the middle of Ebony's back, smiling down at her before looking back at them. "Your sister has proven her loyalty to me, Amber. It is obvious where your own lies."

Amber lifted her chin proudly, "My sister is a fool."

Jerome laughed, leaning down to place a hard kiss on Ebony's bright red lips. "Yes, but at least she will live through this night."

They were going to have to fight their way out of this, but there was no way Chase was going to let Amber die. Not after everything she had done for him. Tightening his arm around her shoulder, he slowly began to gather his power around him, drawing it inside, feeding it and growing it. He was alpha, and had not only his strength, but the strength of his pack bestowed upon him. He would protect what was his, and Amber was his. She was pack, whether she wanted to be or not.

"I leave for a little while, and look what I come back to." Jinx's voice rang out through the darkness, and then he was there, standing between Chase and Jerome. "Ebony," he drawled, "you are looking as conniving and bitchy as ever."

"I'll take that as a compliment."

"You would." *Angel's on her way, Chase. You need to get Amber out of here. Head east as fast as you can, and you will run into them.*

I will not leave you here, Chase growled, aware of the

power now strumming through his veins. *We all go, or no one goes.*

That's not an option, Jinx replied, his gaze never leaving Jerome and Ebony. *Amber is our priority. She is innocent in all of this. We must keep her safe.*

Chase heard someone coming up on one side of them, and then the other. Soon they were surrounded by the General's soldiers. *I will not leave you.*

Chase let his claws lengthen and his fangs drop as he heard, *I can take care of myself.*

I have no doubt that you can, son, but it is my duty and my right to fight beside you.

Why would it be your right?

As an alpha and a father.

There was silence, and then *You aren't my alpha.*

Not yet, but someday, when you are ready to come home, I will be.

"Ebony," Jerome's voice cut through their discussion, "would you like the honor of killing your sister, or should I do it?"

21

Angel and her team moved stealthily through the woods toward the location of the warehouse, communicating through ear coms instead of telepathically so that Sable and Charlotte would be able to hear everything. "Keep your guns ready," she ordered quietly, "I have a bad feeling about this."

As the words 'copy that' echoed throughout the coms, Angel increased her pace, an all-consuming need to get to their destination quickly pushing her hard. *Angel, you need to hurry. They caught Amber helping Chase escape, and they are going to kill her.*

"No," Angel whispered, moving at an all-out run now.

"Angel, slow down. What the hell is going on?" Jaxson asked urgently, trying to keep up with her.

"They are going to kill Amber," she said, forgetting to be quiet in her rush to get to the warehouse. "We have to get there now!"

"Look, I understand your need to help this girl,"

Sapphire broke in, "but we have to be smart about this, Angel. We can't just go in guns blazing."

"It is what we do," Angel growled back, slowing her pace gradually when she realized they were getting closer.

"No," Sapphire countered. "We do our recon first. We have to be smart about this, Angel. That's what you have taught me over the past few weeks. Brains over emotions always, or people get killed."

She was right, and Angel knew it. "Dammit," Angel muttered, slowing her pace even more. "You're right, but this is important, Sapphire. I don't understand it. I don't know if she belongs to Jinx or what is going on, but she matters to him, and I won't let him down. My son needs me, and I am going to be there."

"We will *all* be there," Flame cut in. "Let's do this, but Sapphire is right, let's do it the right way."

"Agreed."

Suddenly Angel felt something she was afraid she would never feel again. "Chase," she whispered softly. Her mate was near. "We're close."

"I see them," Nico said quietly. "Amber and Chase are next to each other, Jinx is in front of them in some kind of standoff with another man and woman. My guess would be the man is Jerome. The woman is Ebony."

"Sapphire and Charlotte, take to the trees, tell us what you see."

It was hell waiting, but finally Angel heard, "There are soldiers all around them. I see a total of ten, but there could be more."

"I count ten, too," Sapphire agreed. "Tell us when to start picking them off, Angel."

Angel crept forward, until she was close enough to

hear the conversation, her eyes on Chase. His entire body was covered in dark bruises and dried blood. He'd lost weight, and his cheeks were sunken in. His head was lowered, and he had one arm around Amber's shoulders, while she seemed to be holding him up with one around his waist. Anger coursed through her as she felt how much he was suffering. *I'm here, Chase,* she whispered into his mind, praying he would hear her. *I'm right here.*

Angel? She heard the hesitancy in his voice, as if he were afraid it wasn't really her.

Yes, it's me.

They want to kill Amber.

It was just like him to think of everyone else before himself. He was standing on the other end of the gun that was pointed at Amber as well, but his only thought was for the girl. *We aren't going to let that happen.*

"You sure you don't want the honors, Ebony?" Angel watched as the man she presumed was Jerome let go of the dark haired beauty next to him, the same one who had kidnapped her babies and Chase, to move closer to Amber. When Jinx stepped in front of him, the man chuckled. "Do you really think to challenge me, pup? For her?" He motioned to Amber, and Angel saw her flinch, before a mask fell over her face. Interesting.

Jinx stood his ground, his hands out to his sides, a low growl of warning crawling up his throat. "She is not to be harmed."

Jerome was quiet for a moment before he asked, "So that's the way it is going to be? You will turn your back on the General? For her?"

"The General isn't here," Jinx growled, "and I don't take orders from you."

"She is under my protection," Chase interrupted, drawing Jerome's attention to him.

"Your protection?" Jerome threw his head back and laughed. "After the sessions we've had lately, I doubt you can even move by yourself, let alone protect anyone."

"You underestimate me," Chase snarled, and Angel watched as he moved in front of Amber. The power flowing around him was phenomenal, literally off the charts. She had never seen power like it from an alpha before.

"Wait," Amber said, trying to push her way between Chase and Jerome. Her gaze went to Jinx, and she shook her head, her large eyes full of sadness. "Don't, please, I'm not worth it."

Angel saw the indecision warring in her son's eyes, before he closed the distance between himself and Amber, and gently pushed her behind him. "To me, you are."

"How fucking pathetic," Ebony drawled, pulling her gun from her waist. "I have more important things to do today than to sit here and watch my daddy's favorite assassin drool over my loser of a sister like the dog that he is." Raising her gun, she looked at Jinx, "You can thank me later." Angel watched in shock as Ebony pulled the trigger, and a bullet lodged in Jerome's chest. "Like Jinx, I take orders from the General. Not you." Then she was gone, as if she'd never been there.

"Now, Sapphire and Charlotte," Angel ordered, her eyes widening in horror when Jerome managed to raise the gun he held and pointed it at Jinx. She was on her feet and running, knowing there was no way she would make it in time, watching in shock at the scene that was unfolding before her.

There was a loud crack and then another, as the gun was fired twice, a gleam of satisfaction in Jerome's eyes as the bullets left the chamber. Chase let out a loud roar, leaping in front of Jinx, taking the bullets meant for him. He clasped a hand around the other man's throat, squeezing tightly. Jerome fought back, but it was useless. Chase raised him off the ground with just one hand by his throat, and the man who had looked too large and mean before was powerless. "No one hurts my family," Chase snarled, before letting go of Jerome, and quickly ending his life with one swipe of his claws.

"Three down," Sapphire reported.

"Four here," Charlotte said.

"What about Ebony?" Angel asked, pulling out her throwing stars and sending them flying at the soldiers closest to her.

"She's gone, boss."

Angel didn't respond as she came to a stop in front of the man she loved, the man she had thought she might never see again. His clear blue eyes met hers as he swayed on his feet, blood pouring from the two wounds in his chest. Wounds he received from protecting her son. He was clothed only in a pair of shredded pants that barely covered him at this point, covered in bruises from head to toe. He was the best thing she had seen in a long time.

"They are all down, boss," Jaxson said, coming up behind her.

She heard him, but she only had eyes for her mate. "I love you, Chase Montgomery," she whispered, uncaring who heard.

His eyes widened in surprise, and he reached out to her, "Love you," he muttered.

She caught him just before he hit the ground, and ended up down there with him. Kissing his forehead, and cheeks, she hollered, "Nico! I need you!"

"Right here, Angel." Nico was beside them instantly, kneeling and opening a First Aid kit.

"Is he going to be okay?" Amber asked, stepping around Jinx, as he wiped the blood from his sword and returned it to the scabbard at his back.

Angel felt for his pulse, smiling through her tears at the strong beat. "Yes, he's going to be just fine."

"Tell him," Amber paused, "tell him thank you, Angel. I don't think he understands how much everything he has done means to me."

"You can tell him yourself," Angel told her. "You are coming home with us."

"I can't," Amber whispered, moisture gathering in her eyes as she slowly backed away from them. "I wish I could, I really do, but my place is here."

"Your place is with us, Amber," Angel corrected her. "With the White River Wolves. We are your family now."

Amber shook her head, tears now streaming down her face. "I can't. There are people that depend on me. I've made promises. I have to keep them."

"Let us help you keep them." Even as the words left her mouth, Angel knew it was a losing battle. Her heart went out to the girl who just wanted to do the right thing.

Jinx knelt next to Angel, his eyes on Chase as he asked, "What about your sister, Amber?"

"Ebony won't hurt me." Angel heard the lie in her voice, scented it in the air, and knew Jinx did, too. "You all don't know what this means to me. I've never had anyone truly care about me. But I can't go with you. People will die if I do, and I just can't live with that." Amber turned and walked away without another word.

"We need to get going, Angel. I've removed the bullets from Chase, but I would feel better if Doc Josie checked him out."

"Me, too," Angel agreed, kissing Chase softly on the lips before rising. "We will need to carry him back to the SUV. We should probably make some kind of stretcher since it is a couple of miles away."

"I've got him," Jinx said, sliding his arms under Chase's back and legs and standing.

"Are you finally coming home, Jinx?" Angel asked softly.

Jinx looked in the direction Amber had gone and shook his head, "Not yet."

Angel nodded. "I understand."

"No, you don't. But you will."

22

Chase groaned, covering his eyes with his forearm as the early morning sunlight streamed in through the curtains. He needed to get his lazy ass out of bed and get into the office, but he was following the doctor's orders. That, and he was too busy pouting. He'd been home for almost a full week, and had only seen Angel twice since he was released from the hospital by Doc Josie after the second day. Not only that, but everything seemed to be running fine without him, because neither his beta nor his head enforcer had stopped by to fill him in on pack activity.

"Daddy, Daddy!" Faith squealed, rushing into the room and jumping on the bed, followed closely by her sister, who still refused to change out of her wolf form. "We are going to the playground. Do you want to come?"

Just hearing the word Daddy from her lips brought tears to his eyes. Before he could answer, Jade swept into the room and gathered Hope into her arms, slipped her fingers into Faith's and tugged her toward the door.

"Daddy needs his rest, girls. We will see him later tonight." With a grin and a wink, Jade left, shutting the door behind them. Well shit, now what? Everyone was acting as if he were made of glass. Except Angel. She was back to acting as if he didn't exist. His dream of hearing her tell him that she loved him must have been that, just a dream.

Sighing, Chase got out of bed and dressed for the day. There was a slight pain in his chest, but he'd shifted several times since they'd gotten home, and he felt almost normal. A little more tired than usual, but Doc Josie said that was to be expected after everything he had gone through. Rubbing his chest absently, Chase left his bedroom and went down to the kitchen for some breakfast. An hour later he was bored as hell, and decided screw the doctor's orders. He was going to work. He needed to take his mind off everything that had happened, he wanted an update on where everything stood with the General, and he wanted to see his damn mate. Where the hell was she?

Deciding to stop at the park and check on the girls on his way to the office, Chase left his house and walked slowly through the compound. It was bright out, and just a little chilly, but that was the way Chase liked it. Not too hot and not too cold. Shoving his hands into the front pockets of his jeans, he rounded the corner of one of the apartment buildings, and stopped in the middle of the sidewalk. His girls were having fun at the playground in front of him, but they were not alone. He swore half of RARE was with them. Phoenix pushed Faith on the swings, while Serenity stood next to him clapping as Hunter pumped his legs and went higher and higher on his own. Nico and Jenna were with Lily on the slides, and

Jade held Hope in her arms nearby. He also noticed that Steele and Storm seemed to stand guard on one side of the playground, while Aiden and Xavier were on the other.

Frowning in confusion, Chase walked over and sat on the bench beside Jade. He let his gaze wander around the compound, noticing the added security features, including cameras and an actual gate that had to be raised before anyone could drive through the front entrance. What the hell had been going on while he was stuck at home? Who had authorized all of this?

"You are supposed to be resting," Jade teased him, stroking the soft fur between Hope's ears.

Chase reached over and took Hope from her, cuddling the pup close. A soft whimper left her muzzle, and Chase whispered, "You are safe, sweetheart. Daddy's here now." Hope looked up at him with wide, sad blue eyes, and he leaned down to kiss her on top of the head before asking, "What's up with all of the security?"

"Angel says it is necessary to protect the pack from the General, and anyone else who wants to threaten us."

Chase glanced around the area again, noticing two of his enforcers in wolf form patrolling near the fence. "This is all Angel's doing?"

Jade smiled, "She's been very busy since you came home."

Yes, it would seem she had. Giving Hope one last kiss, he handed her back to Jade and stood. "Do you know where she is now?"

Before she could reply, he heard someone calling his name. Turning, he was surprised to see Alanna and Fallon walking his way. "Hello, Alpha," Alanna said, smiling at him. “I’m glad you are out and about. We were getting worried.”

“Thank you, Alanna.”

She laughed, her brown eyes sparkling with a hidden humor he hadn’t seen from her before. “You didn’t expect to see us still here, did you?” When he shook his head, she said, “Your wonderful mate got permission from the council for us to stay. She is a woman sent by the Gods.”

“Yes, she is,” Chase agreed, wondering just where the hell his woman was.

Alanna reached out and touched his chest, whispering softly, “May you be free of pain, Alpha, and know how much I appreciate you and yours.”

Chase gasped, wonder filling him as a bright light seemed to enter his chest, moving through his chest, over his arms, then down his waist and legs, until it had swept throughout his entire body, wiping all pain and stiffness left from his captivity in its wake. He looked at Alanna in shock. “What did you do?”

Alanna smiled a gentle smile. “Now you know my secret, Alpha. One I have already shared with Angel. It is why the council sent you to rescue me. In the wrong hands, I am not just a healer, but I could be used as a weapon.”

Chase covered the hand on his chest with his own, smiling in understanding. “Your secret is safe with me, Alanna.”

“I have more secrets,” she whispered, lowering her eyes to the sidewalk.

“They will wait for another day,” he told her.

Nodding, she and Fallon said their goodbyes, and Chase looked around to see if anyone had caught on to what had just happened, but no one seemed to be paying attention. No one except Steele Maddox. He met Steele's gaze, and taking a deep breath, walked over to the other man. Josie had told him that Steele and Storm had refused to leave his daughters' sides while he and Angel were gone, guarding them with their lives. It was something he would expect them to do for Jade, but not Faith and Hope. They may have just been doing their job, but they deserved to be thanked for it.

Chase stopped beside Steele, folding his arms across his chest as he stared at Faith on the swing. "Thank you," he said gruffly, "for taking care of my girls while I was gone."

"It was nothing that you haven't done for me," Steele replied.

Chase turned to look at him, into eyes so much like his son's. "I wanted to bring Jinx home. I failed."

Steele shook his head, "No, Chase, you didn't. You gave my son something he has never had before. Love and acceptance. A place to come home to when he is ready. You were willing to give your life for him. Loving him, even knowing who he is and the life he has been forced to live, is a gift beyond measure. You have failed at nothing."

Steele held out a hand to him, and after a moment Chase clasped it with his own. "We will bring him home someday."

"Yes," Steele agreed, "we will."

Saying goodbye, Chase left, crossing the street to his office building. So much had happened since he'd been taken, that it was a lot to take in. And it all seemed to be centered around Angel. She had done numerous things for not only her team, but his pack. Giving of herself, just as an Alpha's mate should.

Lost in thought, he opened the door to his office, and froze. There, sitting behind his desk in his black leather chair, was his beautiful mate. Her long blonde hair flowed freely down her back, her intense blue gaze on the woman in front of her as she said, "Jaxson has done a background check, and as far as I can tell everything is legit on this one, but I want you to personally check it out before we accept the mission from the council, Sable. Take one of the other enforcers with you."

"Are you sure?" Sable responded. "Chase normally likes to check everything out himself first."

Angel's gaze left hers and connected with his, a small smile crossing her lips. "Your alpha is going to be busy for the next few days. Look into it, get back to myself or Chase with your opinion, but don't be gone too long. One of the council members will be here on the next full moon, and I expect you to be back by then."

"Yes, Angel," Sable said, rising. "Thank you for trusting me with something like this. I will take Aiden with me, if you approve."

"Of course." Chase was surprised to see Angel get up and come around the desk, giving Sable a quick hug. "Be safe."

Sable returned her embrace before turning toward him. "I hope you are feeling better, Alpha."

"I am." And he was. He felt remarkably well after everything he'd been through, thanks to Alanna and whatever healing powers she possessed. "I will see you when you get back from your mission, Sable."

With a grin of anticipation, Sable nodded and left the

room. Chase slammed the door behind her, turning the lock before facing Angel. "You've been running from me."

"Never again," she promised.

Chase frowned, "You haven't been to see me in days."

"I was taking care of things here so that you could rest...and I was waiting."

"What the fuck for?" he growled, slowly stalking toward her. He was done waiting. She was his, dammit, and it was time she realized that.

He saw the excited gleam in her eyes before she responded, "For you."

Chase could not stop the low growl from erupting, and he knew his eyes had gone wolf. His sharp fangs lengthened, biting into his bottom lip. Stopping in front of her, he slipped his fingers into her hair, fisting it to hold her still. "Tell me again," he growled. "I need to hear it."

He did not have to say what it was that he needed to hear. Angel already knew. Her features softened and she leaned into him. "I love you, Chase Montgomery. I am yours, now and forever. Heart and soul."

Chase's eyes went to her neck, and he couldn't look away. The need to mark her, to claim her as his, clawed at his insides. The zipper of his jeans bit into his hard, straining cock, and he wanted to sink balls deep into the beauty in front of him. "We need to go home where I can do this right," he rasped, giving into the need to stroke his tongue down the length of her neck, gently raking his fangs over the soft skin. "Fuck, we need to go now before I take you here on my desk."

Angel tilted her head to the side, sliding her fingers

into his thick, dark hair and pulling him closer, "I don't need a bed, Chase. I need my mate. Now!"

Chase snarled loudly, opening his mouth wide over her shoulder, his whole body shaking with the need to claim what was his. He ground his aching dick into her, groaning as he slipped a hand under her shirt and up, over her soft skin to cup her breast.

"Chase, please." He couldn't hold back any longer. As much as he wanted to take the time to worship her body like it deserved, there was no way he would be able to wait.

"Are you sure?" He would give her one last chance, even though he knew it was futile.

Angel leaned back, her light blue eyes lit with need. "Yes."

One word, so short and simple. It was all he needed. Sliding his hands down, he quickly undid her jeans, slipping them from her legs along with her panties. His jeans quickly followed, along with her shirt. Not giving a shit what was on his desk, he reached behind her and shoved it all on the floor. Grasping her hips, he lifted her and gently sat her on the surface of the cherry wood. Leaning down, he traced her lips with his tongue before shoving past them and claiming her mouth with his. He wanted to be gentle, he really did, but a year was a long time to go without claiming your mate.

I don't need gentle, Angel whispered into his mind. *I don't want it. I want you, Chase, deep inside me. I want it hard, and I want it fast. I need it. I need to feel you alive, in me, over me, biting me.*

It was exactly what he needed, and he was done fighting it. Grasping Angel's hips, he pulled her to the edge of the desk, guiding his cock to her entrance, and sliding deep into the slick hotness. He shuddered when she wrapped her legs around his waist, pulling him even deeper.

"Chase," she gasped, lying back on the desk and tilting her hips up. "That feels so good. So right."

"Yes," he agreed through clenched teeth, his eyes on the sight before him. She was so damn beautiful, laid out in front of him. Her pert breasts rose with every ragged breath she took, her golden skin so soft, her back arching off the table as she pushed closer to him. She was so gorgeous, and she was all his. Finally.

With a firm hold on her hips, Chase began to move, sinking deep inside her, before pulling back, and then doing it again. He couldn't get enough. She was so hot, so wet, so tight. He moved faster and faster, low growls of pure lust rising from his throat, the need to bite her pushing at him. "Angel," he growled, "there's no going back. You are mine."

Her eyes opened, glowing brightly with pleasure, and she raised up off the table, baring her neck for him. "I've always been yours."

The words had no sooner left her lips, than Chase covered her shoulder with his mouth, sinking his fangs deep. "Mine," he grunted around his fangs, holding on tightly to her. "Mine."

Angel threw her head back, crying out as she came hard. Then she found her mating bite on his neck and bit down hard. He came instantly, breathing heavily as he continued to pound deep inside of her until he was spent, his mate's voice echoing in his mind. *Mine!*

Angel held Chase close, refusing to remove her fangs from him. Suddenly she was enveloped with a feeling of warmth and happiness, and she literally felt their souls unite as one. Then came the power, more than she'd ever felt before, washing into her, surrounding her, then settling deep inside, as if waiting until it was needed. There was so much of it that she could not hold back her gasp of stunned surprise.

Chase gently removed his teeth, licking at the mate bite, before placing gentle kisses over it. A tremor ran through her at the sensual feel of his mouth against her skin, and she removed her fangs to return the favor.

"I love you, Angel Johnston," Chase said quietly. "I always have, and I always will."

Angel smiled at him, tracing his face with her fingertips. "We are one now, my love. United, and stronger than ever, just like you said we would be. I feel the power inside me. I feel you, your strength and wisdom."

"The power comes not only from us, but from the pack," Chase explained, kissing her fingers as she brushed his lips with them. "As my Alpha mate, you share that power with me."

"I had no idea," Angel confessed. While she had felt some power from her team as their alpha, this was so much more.

"I don't expect your team to accept me as their alpha."

"They already do," Angel told him.

"They do? All of them?"

"Yes," Angel said, sliding her fingers into his hair and pulling him close. "On the next full moon, one of the council members will be here to facilitate our mating ceremony. At that time, all members of my team, along with Alanna and Fallon, will be officially accepted as a part of the pack."

"You've been busy, my mate," Chase growled, lowering his head to lick his mark again.

"Yes," Angel whispered breathlessly, arching into his touch as his fingers skated over her body.

"I think I am going to keep you very busy in the future," Chase rasped, shoving deep inside her again as he bit down.

Angel screamed, unable to hold back, as she raked her claws down his back. "Chase!"

"Very busy," he groaned.

23

Three days later, Chase and Angel stood under the full moon, facing each other. They had just completed the ritual that bound her team, along with Alanna and Fallon, to the White River Wolves, making them a part of the pack. Now it was time for their mating ceremony, but Chase felt the sadness in his mate. She looked up at him, trying to hide her emotions behind a brilliant smile, but he knew better. There was a part of her missing tonight, on a night that should have been one of the happiest in her life, and she felt it deeply.

She was dressed in a long white gown, the same one his mother had worn when she mated his father so long ago. The same one Jenna wore in her mating ceremony with Nico. It was a tradition in their family, and it had meant the world to him when Angel agreed to wear it. Her hair was left loose, falling down her back in gentle curls, with a wreath of white roses adorning her head. She wore a blue necklace that matched the color of her eyes, and a matching ankle bracelet, her feet bare. She was exquisite, and Chase could not wait to have her to himself. But first, they needed to finish the mating ceremony. And that could not happen just yet.

Council Elder Jacques Moreau stood in front of them dressed in a long white robe, holding the ceremonial knife. Jade, Faith, and Hope stood beside Angel. Jade held Hope close, the child still in her wolf form. No matter what Chase and Angel tried, she still refused to shift. Chase looked down into Angel's eyes, overwhelmed by the love he felt for her. They were surrounded by family and friends, but still, one person was missing. And he was going to do everything in his power to fix that.

"Chase, Angel," the council elder said, with a small smile, "are you ready?"

"Not yet," Chase responded, reaching out to gently run a hand down Angel's hair, before cupping her cheek. "I will be right back, my love." Her eyes widened in surprise, but she nodded.

Ignoring the curious stares of his wolves, Chase left the clearing where everyone was gathered and quickly made his way through the trees and up a steep incline. He found what he was searching for at the top. "I'm glad you could make it, son."

Jinx stared out over the land below, at where the three small fires were lit for the ceremony. "How did you know I was up here?"

"I felt you."

Jinx turned, his eyes narrowed on him, "That's impossible. I was masking my presence. Not even my dad or Angel knows I'm here."

Chase shrugged, "You must not have been hiding from me then." When Jinx glanced back down at the flicker of flames below, Chase took a step toward him. "Why don't you come join the ceremony?"

"I can't do that."

"Why not?"

"I wouldn't be welcome," Jinx said shortly. "I would ruin it for you. No one wants me there."

"Not true, Jinx. Angel does, and so do I. Your sisters, your father, your aunt and uncle. We all want you there."

Chase saw the battle Jinx was fighting before he whispered, "I've never been wanted before."

Chase walked slowly forward, then rested a hand gently on the young man's shoulder. "You *are* wanted, Jinx."

"If the pack sees me, the General could find out."

"My wolves will keep your secret if I tell them to. But what if he does find out? Worst case scenario, you come home, where you belong."

They stood in silence for a moment before Jinx finally nodded. "We better go. Angel's getting worried."

Chase laughed, "She's probably thinking of ways to run, but it is too late for that."

Jinx grinned, his white teeth flashing in the night. "Way too late."

When Chase and Jinx entered the clearing just moments later, Chase felt the tension rise not only in the man next to him, but in everyone else. Raising his voice, he declared, "This is Steele and Angel's son, Jinx. I claim him as my own son. He is a member of this pack, even if he does not choose to officially become a part of it right now. You will show him the respect an alpha's son deserves."

Pride filled him when every member of his pack immediately knelt to one knee, bowing their head, accepting Jinx unconditionally as one of their own, and as his son. When they rose, he nodded to them, allowing the love he felt for them all to shine in his eyes. Chase walked through the middle of the large throng of people, Jinx at his side, his eyes on his mate. Hers were wide, filled with tears and love for him.

When Jinx paused suddenly, Chase glanced over to see him staring at little Hope. Jade held her close, but the young pup still shivered in fear. "It's not you, Jinx," Chase said quietly. "She's been like that ever since the General took them. The trauma of going back into the hell they had escaped last year was too much for her. She refuses to shift back."

Jinx cocked his head to one side as if in thought, then slowly approached Hope. "Hey, little sister," he said softly. When Hope whimpered, he reached out to stroke his hand gently down her back. "You know who I am?" Hope's ears perked forward, as she listened intently. "I'm your big brother. You know what that means? I will protect you with my life. I won't let anyone, and I mean anyone, hurt you again." When Hope whined plaintively, he whispered, "I know it is scary, little one, but you are safe."

Chase watched in awe as a soft light enveloped Hope, and then she seemed to shimmer, right before she shifted back into the sweet baby girl he'd missed so much. Chase accepted a blanket from one of his wolves and wrapped the little girl in it, holding her close. "It's nice to have you back, baby."

Hope's big eyes went from him to Jinx. "You promise?" she whispered to Jinx.

"I promise," he vowed solemnly.

Hope nodded in satisfaction, "Someone like you doesn't break promises."

"Someone like me?"

"Yes, a brother. You protect people. Like Jade. You kept her safe, and you will keep me and Faith safe, too."

"You better believe it," Jinx said roughly, his eyes widening in shock when Hope held out her arms to him. He glanced at Chase as if asking for permission, and Chase simply handed his daughter to him.

"Come on, son. Your mother is waiting."

When Jinx moved as if to stand beside Steele, Chase shook his head. "I know Steele is your father, but you are a part of our family, too, and you belong with us."

"He's right," Steele said, clapping his son on the back. "Go stand with Chase, Jinx."

Jinx glanced around the clearing quickly, looking at all of the expectant gazes, before agreeing quietly. It was obvious that he was uneasy with all of the attention, but he cuddled Hope close and stood stiffly by Chase.

The council elder smiled, raising his head to include everyone, "Shall we begin now?"

It was close to dawn when Angel fell into bed beside Chase. She was happy, and felt blessed beyond measure. She could not have asked for anything more than she had right now, except for Jinx to be home to live with them. But he had insisted on going back to D.C., saying the fight was not over yet, and he was still needed on the inside. She'd seen the way he looked at his sisters though, and hope filled her that he would not be gone long. He was beginning to understand what it was like to have a family, one who loved you unconditionally and would do anything for you. And she could tell that taste of what could be affected him more than he let on.

And Rikki. Angel had missed her friend at the ceremony tonight. Doc Josie had assured her that Rikki was doing just fine. She was resting now, and would hopefully awaken soon. Which meant Angel and her team needed to find Jeremiah fast. Who knew what would happen if Rikki woke after all this time, just to find out that her mate infiltrated the General's army, and was working on bringing him down from the inside? Angel didn't even want to think about it. Not after everything she had just gone through with her own mate. No, they would find Jeremiah and bring him home before Rikki even knew he'd been gone. Then when her friend joined the land of the living again, it would be with her mate at her side, as it was supposed to be.

"What are you smiling about, Mrs. Montgomery," Chase asked, nuzzling her neck with his nose as he ran a hand over her now naked body.

"Life," she whispered, pushing him over and straddling him. "It's good right now."

She felt his thick cock nudge against her entrance before he gripped her hips, lifting her and settling her on top of him. "Yes," he groaned, "it is good." Taking her nipple into his mouth, he bit it lightly, before stroking it with his tongue. "Really good."

Angel moaned, running her hands down his chest as she whispered, "I love you, Chase."

Chase flipped her over, hovering over her as he began to push in and out of her tight channel. Threading his fingers through her hair, he gripped it lightly as he captured her lips with his. "Love you, baby."

24

Jinx strode down the long corridor of the facility in D.C., nodding at soldiers he passed on the way. He still could not believe that not only had Chase Montgomery accepted him as his son, but so had his entire pack. It had made him uncomfortable because he wasn't used to being around a lot of people at once, but it also made him feel something else. A part of something he had never felt before. Family. Yes, he'd had his sister Jade, and his father, but he hardly ever saw them. He loved them the best he knew how, was willing to die for them both. But until last night, he never understood what it was like to be a part of something so large.

His steps faltered when he thought of little Hope. She had placed her trust in him, trusting him to watch over her like he did Jade when they were growing up. And Faith felt the same way. In their minds, it was what big brothers did, and there was no doubt on their end that he would protect them like he did Jade. The responsibility was overwhelming, but he could handle it. He would. For his sisters...for his family.

Stopping outside a room on the lower level of the large building, he stared into the room through a small glass window at the man who lay in the hospital bed. The one person who threatened everything he held close to his heart. If he thought it would keep his sisters safe, he would end the General's life right now. Unfortunately, he was just one man in a much larger operation, as was proven when Jerome was sent to them. He'd been working hard to find out who the main person in charge was, but even though he was able to locate several others higher up in the chain of command than the General, the answer still evaded him. It wouldn't for long though, and once he knew, he would tear the entire thing down piece by piece. He wasn't alone now. Someone was working on the inside with him. Someone the General would never suspect. And soon, if Jinx had his way, it was all going to come crashing down.

Make sure and visit my website for information on all of my books, and to sign up for my Newsletter where you will receive all of the latest information on new releases, sales, and more!

Website: **http://www.dawnsullivanauthor.com/**

I would love to have you join my reader's group, Author Dawn Sullivan's RARE Rebels, so that we can hang out and chat, and where you will also get sneak peeks of cover reveals, read excerpts before anyone else, and more!

https://www.facebook.com/groups/AuthorDawnSullivansRebelReaders/

Dawn Sullivan

ABOUT THE AUTHOR

Dawn Sullivan has a wonderful, supportive husband, and three beautiful children. She enjoys spending time with them, which normally involves some baseball, shooting hoops, taking walks, watching movies, and reading.

Her passion for reading began at a very young age and only grew over time. Whether she was bringing home a book from the library, or sneaking one of her mother's romance novels to read by the light in the hallway when she was supposed to be sleeping, Dawn always had a book. She reads several different genres and subgenres, but Paranormal Romance and Romantic Suspense are her favorites.

Dawn has always made up stories of her own, and finally decided to start sharing them with others. She hopes everyone enjoys reading them as much as she enjoys writing them.

facebook.com/dawnsullivanauthor

twitter.com/dawn_author

instagram.com/dawn_sullivan_author

OTHER BOOKS BY DAWN SULLIVAN

RARE Series

Book 1 Nico's Heart

Book 2 Phoenix's Fate

Book 3 Trace's Temptation

Book 4 Saving Storm

Book 5 Angel's Destiny

White River Wolves Series

Book 1 Josie's Miracle

Book 2 Slade's Desire

Book 3 Janie's Salvation

Serenity Springs Series

Book 1 Tempting His Heart

Book 2 Healing Her Spirit

Book 3 Saving His Soul

Book 4 A Caldwell Wedding

Chosen By Destiny

Book 1 Blayke